IMPOSSIBLE THINGS

IMPOSSIBLE THINGS

CLIFFORD D. SIMAK

WILDSIDE PRESS

CONTENTS

THE WORLD THAT COULDN'T BE

I

The tracks went up one row and down another, and in those rows the *vua* plants had been sheared off an inch or two above the ground. The raider had been methodical; it had not wandered about haphazardly, but had done an efficient job of harvesting the first ten rows on the west side of the field. Then, having eaten its fill, it had angled off into the bush—and that had not been long ago, for the soil still trickled down into the great paw marks, sunk deep into the finely cultivated loam.

Somewhere a sawmill bird was whirring through a log, and down in one of the thorn-choked ravines, a choir of chatterers was clicking through a ghastly morning song. It was going to be a scorcher of a day. Already the smell of desiccated dust was rising from the ground and the glare of the newly risen sun was dancing off the bright leaves of the hula-trees, making it appear as if the bush were filled with a million flashing mirrors.

Gavin Duncan hauled a red bandanna from his pocket and mopped his face.

"No, mister," pleaded Zikkara, the native foreman of the farm. "You cannot do it, mister. You do not hunt a Cytha."

"The hell I don't," said Duncan, but he spoke in English and not the native tongue.

He stared out across the bush, a flat expanse of sun-cured grass interspersed with thickets of hula-scrub and thorn and occasional groves of trees, criss-crossed by treacherous ravines and spotted with infrequent waterholes.

It would be murderous out there, he told himself, but it shouldn't take too long. The beast probably would lay up shortly after its pre-dawn feeding, and he'd overhaul it in an hour or two. But if he failed to overhaul it, then he must keep on.

"Dangerous," Zikkara pointed out. "No one hunts the Cytha."

"I do," Duncan said, speaking now in the native language. "I hunt anything that damages my crop. A few nights more of this and there would be nothing left."

Jamming the bandanna back into his pocket, he tilted his hat lower across his eyes against the sun.

"It might be a long chase, mister. It is the *skun* season now. If you were caught out there. . . ."

"Now listen," Duncan told it sharply. "Before I came, you'd feast one day, then starve for days on end; but now you eat each day. And you like the doctoring. Before, when you got sick, you died. Now you get sick, I doctor you, and you live. You like staying in one place, instead of wandering all around."

"Mister, we like all this," said Zikkara, "but we do not hunt the Cytha."

"If we do not hunt the Cytha, we lose all this," Duncan pointed out. "If I don't make a crop, I'm licked. I'll have to go away. Then what happens to you?"

"We will grow the corn ourselves."

"That's a laugh," said Duncan, "and you know it is. If I didn't kick your backsides all day long, you wouldn't do a lick of work. If I leave, you go back to the bush. Now let's go and get that Cytha."

"But it is such a little one, mister! It is such a young one! It is scarcely worth the trouble. It would be a shame to kill it."

Probably just slightly smaller than a horse, thought Duncan, watching the native closely. It's scared, he told himself. It's scared dry and spitless.

"Besides, it must have been most hungry. Surely, mister, even a Cytha has the right to eat."

"Not from my crop," said Duncan savagely. "You know why we grow the *vua*, don't you? You know it is great medicine. The berries that it grows cures those who are sick inside their heads. My people need that medicine—need it very badly. And what is more, out there—" He swept his arm toward the sky.— "out there they pay very much for it."

"But, mister. . . ."

"I tell you this," said Duncan gently, "you either dig me up a bush-runner to do the tracking for me, or you can all get out, the kit and caboodle of you. I can get other tribes to work the farm."

"No, mister!" Zikkara screamed in desperation.

"You have your choice," Duncan told it coldly.

He plodded back across the field toward the house. Not much of a house as yet. Not a great deal better than a native shack. But someday it would be, he told himself. Let him sell a crop or two, and he'd build a house that would really be a house. It would have a bar and swimming pool and a garden filled with flowers, and at last, after years of wandering, he'd have a home and broad acres and everyone, not just one lousy tribe, would call him mister.

Gavin Duncan, planter, he said to himself, and he liked the sound of it. Planter on the planet Layard. But not if the Cytha came back night after night and ate the *vua* plants.

He glanced over his shoulder and saw Zikkara racing for the native village.

Called their bluff, Duncan informed himself with satisfaction.

He came out of the field and walked across the yard, heading for the house. One of Shotwell's shirts was hanging on the clothes-line, limp in the breathless morning.

Damn the man, thought Duncan. Out here mucking around with those stupid natives, always asking questions, always under foot. Although, to be fair about it, that was Shotwell's job. That was what the Sociology people had sent him out to do.

Duncan came up to the shack, pushed the door open, and entered. Shotwell, stripped to the waist, was at the wash bench. Breakfast was cooking on the stove, with an elderly native acting as cook.

Duncan strode across the room and took down the heavy rifle from its peg. He slapped the action open, slapped it shut again.

Shotwell reached for a towel.

"What's going on?" he asked.

"Cytha got into the field."

"Cytha?"

"A kind of animal," said Duncan. "It ate ten rows of *vua*."

"Big? Little? What are its characteristics?"

The native began putting breakfast on the table. Duncan walked to the table, laid the rifle across one corner of it, and sat down. He poured a brackish liquid out of a big stew pan into their cups.

God, he thought, what I would give for a cup of coffee.

Shotwell pulled up his chair. "You didn't answer me. What is a Cytha like?"

"I wouldn't know," said Duncan.

"Don't know? But you're going after it, looks like, and how can you hunt it if you don't know—"

"Track it. The thing tied to the other end of the trail is sure to be the Cytha. Well find out what it's like once we catch up to it."

"We?"

"The natives will send up someone to do the tracking for me. Some of them are better than a dog."

"Look, Gavin. I've put you to a lot of trouble, and you've been decent with me. If I can be any help, I would like to go."

"Two make better time than three. And we have to catch this Cytha fast or it might settle down to an endurance contest."

"All right, then. Tell me about the Cytha."

Duncan poured porridge gruel into his bowl, handed the pan to Shotwell. "It's a sort of special thing. The natives are scared to death of it. You hear a lot of stories about it. Said to be unkillable. It's always capitalized, always a proper noun. It has been reported at different times from widely scattered places."

"No one's ever bagged one?"

"Not that I ever heard of." Duncan patted the rifle. "Let me get a bead on it, though, and we'll see."

He started eating, spooning the porridge into his mouth, munching on the stale cornbread left from the night before. He drank some of the brackish beverage and shuddered.

"Some day," he said, "I'm going to scrape together enough money to buy a pound of coffee. You'd think—"

"It's the freight rates," Shotwell said. "I'll send you a pound when I go back."

"Not at the price they'd charge to ship it out," said Duncan. "I wouldn't hear of it."

They ate in silence for a time. Finally Shotwell said: "I'm getting nowhere, Gavin. The natives are willing to talk, but it all adds up to nothing."

"I tried to tell you that. You could have saved your time."

Shotwell shook his head stubbornly. "There's an answer, a logical explanation. It's easy enough to say you cannot rule out the sexual factor, but that's exactly what has happened here on Layard. It's easy to exclaim that a sexless animal, a sexless race, a sexless planet is impossible, but that is what we have. Somewhere there is an answer and I have to find it."

"Now hold up a minute," Duncan protested. "There's no use blowing a gasket. I haven't got the time this morning to listen to your lecture."

"But it's not the lack of sex that worries me entirely," Shotwell said, "although it's the central factor. There are subsidiary situations deriving from that central fact which are most intriguing."

"I have no doubt of it," said Duncan, "but if you please—"

"Without sex, there is no basis for the family, and without the family there is no basis for a tribe, and yet the natives have an elaborate tribal setup, with taboos by way of regulation. Somewhere there must exist some underlying, basic unifying factor, some common loyalty, some strange relationship which spells out to brotherhood."

"Not brotherhood," said Duncan, chuckling. "Not even sisterhood. You must watch your terminology. The word you want is ithood."

The door pushed open and a native walked in timidly.

"Zikkara said that mister want me," the native told them. "I am Sipar. I can track anything but screamers, stilt-birds, longhorns and donovans. Those are my taboos."

"I am glad to hear that," Duncan replied. "You have no Cytha taboo, then."

"Cytha!" yipped the native. "Zikkara did not tell me Cytha!"

Duncan paid no attention. He got up from the table and went to the heavy chest that stood against one wall. He rummaged in it and came out with a pair of binoculars, a hunting knife, and an extra drum of ammunition. At the kitchen cupboard, he rummaged once again, filling a small leather sack with a gritty powder from a can he found.

"Rockahominy," he explained to Shotwell. "Emergency rations thought up by the primitive North American Indians. Parched corn, ground fine. It's no feast exactly, but it keeps a man going."

"You figure you'll be gone that long?"

"Maybe overnight. I don't know. Won't stop until I get it. Can't afford to. It could wipe me out in a few days."

"Good hunting," Shotwell said. "I'll hold the fort."

Duncan said to Sipar: "Quit sniveling and come on."

He picked up the rifle, settled it in the crook of his arm. He kicked open the door and strode out.

Sipar followed meekly.

II

Duncan got his first shot late in the afternoon of that first day.

In the middle of the morning, two hours after they had left the farm, they had flushed the Cytha out of its bed in a thick ravine. But there had been no chance for a shot. Duncan saw no more than a huge black blur fade into the bush.

Through the bake-oven afternoon, they had followed its trail, Sipar tracking and Duncan bringing up the rear, scanning every piece of cover, with the sun-hot rifle always held at ready.

Once they had been held up for fifteen minutes while a massive donovan tramped back and forth, screaming, trying to work up its courage for attack. But after a quarter hour of showing off, it decided to behave itself and went off at a shuffling gallop.

Duncan watched it go with a lot of thankfulness. It could soak up a lot of lead, and for all its awkwardness, it was handy with its feet once it set itself in motion. Donovans had killed a lot of men in the twenty years since Earthmen had come to Layard.

With the beast gone, Duncan looked around for Sipar. He found it fast asleep beneath a hula-shrub. He kicked the native awake with something less than gentleness, and they went on again.

The bush swarmed with other animals, but they had no trouble with them.

Sipar, despite its initial reluctance, had worked well at the trailing. A misplaced bunch of grass, a twig bent to one side, a displaced stone, the faintest paw mark were Sipar's stock in trade. It worked like a lithe, well-trained hound. This bush country was its special province; here it was at home.

With the sun dropping toward the west, they had climbed a long, steep hill, and as they neared the top of it, Duncan hissed at Sipar. The native looked back over its shoulder in surprise. Duncan made motions for it to stop tracking.

The native crouched, and as Duncan went past it, he saw that a look of agony was twisting its face. And in the look of agony he thought he saw as well a touch of pleading and a trace of hatred. It's scared, just like the rest of them, Duncan told himself. But what the native thought or felt had no significance; what counted was the beast ahead.

Duncan went the last few yards on his belly, pushing the gun ahead of him, the binoculars bumping on his back. Swift, vicious insects ran out of the grass and swarmed across his hands and arms and one got on his face and bit him.

He made it to the hilltop and lay there, looking at the sweep of land beyond. It was more of the same, more of the blistering, dusty slogging, more of thorn and tangled ravine and awful emptiness.

He lay motionless, watching for a hint of motion, for the fitful shadow, for any wrongness in the terrain that might be the Cytha.

But there was nothing. The land lay quiet under the declining sun. Far on the horizon, a herd of some sort of animals was grazing, but there was nothing else.

Then he saw the motion, just a flicker, on the knoll ahead—about halfway up.

He laid the rifle carefully on the ground and hitched the binoculars around. He raised them to his eyes and moved them slowly back and forth. The animal was there where he had seen the motion.

It was resting, looking back along the way that it had come, watching for the first sign of its trailers. Duncan tried to make out the size and shape, but it blended with the grass and the dun soil, and he could not be sure exactly what it looked like.

He let the glasses down, and now that he had located it, he could distinguish its outline with the naked eye.

His hand reached out and slid the rifle to him. He fitted it to his shoulder and wriggled his body for closer contact with the ground. The cross-hairs centered on the faint outline on the knoll, and then the beast stood up.

It was not as large as he had thought it might be—perhaps a little larger than Earth-lion size—but it certainly was no lion. It was a square-set thing and black and inclined to lumpiness, and it had an awkward look about it, but there were strength and ferociousness as well.

Duncan tilted the muzzle of the rifle so that the cross-hairs centered on the massive neck. He drew in a breath and held it and began the trigger squeeze.

The rifle bucked hard against his shoulder and the report hammered in his head and the beast went down. It did not lurch or fall; it simply melted down and disappeared, hidden in the grass.

"Dead center," Duncan assured himself.

He worked the mechanism, and the spent cartridge case flew out. The feeding mechanism snicked, and the fresh shell clicked as it slid into the breech.

He lay for a moment, watching. And on the knoll where the thing had fallen, the grass was twitching as if the wind were blowing, only there was no wind. But despite the twitching of the grass, there was no sign of the Cytha. It did not struggle up again. It stayed where it had fallen.

Duncan got to his feet, dug out the bandanna and mopped at his face. He heard the soft thud of the step behind him and turned his head. It was the tracker.

"It's all right, Sipar," he said. "You can quit worrying. I got it. We can go home now."

It had been a long, hard chase, longer than he had thought it might be. But it had been successful, and that was the thing that counted. For the moment, the *vua* crop was safe.

He tucked the bandanna back into his pocket, went down the slope, and started up the knoll. He reached the place where the Cytha had fallen. There were three small gouts of torn, mangled fur and flesh lying on the ground, and there was nothing else.

He spun around and jerked his rifle up. Every nerve was screamingly alert. He swung his head, searching for the slightest movement, for some shape or color that was not the shape or color of the bush or grass or ground. But there was nothing. The heat droned in the hush of afternoon. There was not a breath of moving air. But there was danger—a saw-toothed sense of danger close behind his neck.

"Sipar!" he called in a tense whisper, "Watch out!"

The native stood motionless, unheeding, its eyeballs rolling up until there was only white, while the muscles stood out along its throat like straining ropes of steel.

Duncan slowly swiveled, rifle held almost at arm's length, elbows crooked a little, ready to bring the weapon into play in a fraction of a second.

Nothing stirred. There was no more than emptiness—the emptiness of sun and molten sky, of grass and scraggy bush, of a brown-and-yellow land stretching into foreverness.

Step by step, Duncan covered the hillside and finally came back to the place where the native squatted on its heels and moaned, rocking back and forth, arms locked tightly across its chest, as if it tried to cradle itself in a sort of illusory comfort.

The Earthman walked to the place where the Cytha had fallen and picked up, one by one, the bits of bleeding flesh. They had been mangled by his bullet. They were limp and had no shape. And it was queer, he thought. In all his years of hunting, over many planets, he had never known a bullet to rip out hunks of flesh.

He dropped the bloody pieces back into the grass and wiped his hand upon his thighs. He got up a little stiffly.

He'd found no trail of blood leading through the grass, and surely an animal with a hole of that size would leave a trail.

And as he stood there upon the hillside, with the bloody fingerprints still wet and glistening upon the fabric of his trousers, he felt the first cold touch of fear, as if the fingertips of fear might momentarily, almost casually, have trailed across his heart.

He turned around and walked back to the native, reached down and shook it.

"Snap out of it," he ordered.

He expected pleading, cowering, terror, but there was none.

Sipar got swiftly to its feet and stood looking at him and there was, he thought, an odd glitter in its eyes.

"Get going," Duncan said. "We still have a little time. Start circling and pick up the trail. I will cover you."

He glanced at the sun. An hour and a half still left—maybe as much as two. There might still be time to get this buttoned up before the fall of night.

* * * *

A half mile beyond the knoll, Sipar picked up the trail again, and they went ahead, but now they traveled more cautiously, for any bush, any rock, any clump of grass might conceal the wounded beast.

Duncan found himself on edge and cursed himself savagely for it. He'd been in tight spots before. This was nothing new to him. There was no reason to get himself tensed up. It was a deadly business, sure, but he had faced others calmly and walked away from them. It was those frontier tales he'd heard about the Cytha—the kind of superstitious chatter that one always heard on the edge of unknown land.

He gripped the rifle tighter and went on.

No animal, he told himself, was unkillable.

Half an hour before sunset, he called a halt when they reached a brackish waterhole. The light soon would be getting bad for shooting. In the morning, they'd take up the trail again, and by that time the Cytha would be at an even greater disadvantage. It would be stiff and slow and weak. It might be even dead.

Duncan gathered wood and built a fire in the lee of a thornbush thicket. Sipar waded out with the canteens and thrust them at arm's length beneath the surface to fill them. The water still was warm and evil-tasting, but it was fairly free of scum, and a thirsty man could drink it.

The sun went down and darkness fell quickly. They dragged more wood out of the thicket and piled it carefully close at hand.

Duncan reached into his pocket and brought out the little bag of rockahominy.

"Here," he said to Sipar. "Supper."

The native held one hand cupped and Duncan poured a little mound into its palm.

"Thank you, mister," Sipar said. "Food-giver."

"Huh?" asked Duncan, then caught what the native meant. "Dive into it," he said, almost kindly. "It isn't much, but it gives you strength. We'll need strength tomorrow."

Food-giver, eh? Trying to butter him up, perhaps. In a little while, Sipar would start whining for him to knock off the hunt and head back for the farm.

Although, come to think of it, he really was the food-giver to this bunch of sexless wonders. Corn, thank God, grew well on the red and stubborn soil of Layard—good old corn from North America. Fed to hogs, made into corn-pone for breakfast back on Earth, and here, on Layard, the staple food crop for a gang of shiftless varmints who still regarded, with some good solid skepticism and round-eyed wonder, this unorthodox idea that one should take the trouble to grow plants to eat rather than go out and scrounge for them.

Corn from North America, he thought, growing side by side with the *vua* of Layard. And that was the way it went. Something from one planet and something from another and still something further from a third and so was built up through the wide social confederacy of space a truly cosmic culture which in the end, in another ten thousand years or so, might spell out some way of life with more sanity and understanding than was evident today.

He poured a mound of rockahominy into his own hand and put the bag back into his pocket.

"Sipar."

"Yes, mister?"

"You were not scared today when the donovan threatened to attack us."

"No, mister. The donovan would not hurt me."

"I see. You said the donovan was taboo to you. Could it be that you, likewise, are taboo to the donovan?"

"Yes, mister. The donovan and I grew up together."

"Oh, so that's it," said Duncan.

He put a pinch of the parched and powdered corn into his mouth and took a sip of brackish water. He chewed reflectively on the resultant mash.

He might go ahead, he knew, and ask why and how and where Sipar and the donovan had grown up together, but there was no point to it. This was exactly the kind of tangle that Shotwell was forever getting into.

Half the time, he told himself, I'm convinced the little stinkers are doing no more than pulling our legs. What a fantastic bunch of jerks! Not men, not women, just things. And while there were never babies, there were children, although never less than eight or nine years old. And if there were no babies, where did the eight- and nine-year-olds come from?

"I suppose," he said, "that these other things that are your ta-boos, the stilt-birds and the screamers and the like, also grew up with you."

"That is right, mister."

"Some playground that must have been," said Duncan.

He went on chewing, staring out into the darkness beyond the ring of firelight.

"There's something in the thorn bush, mister."

"I didn't hear a thing."

"Little pattering. Something is running there."

Duncan listened closely. What Sipar said was true. A lot of little things were running in the thicket.

"More than likely mice," he said.

He finished his rockahominy and took an extra swig of water, gagging on it slightly.

"Get your rest," he told Sipar. "I'll wake you later so I can catch a wink or two."

"Mister," Sipar said, "I will stay with you to the end."

"Well," said Duncan, somewhat startled, "that is decent of you."

"I will stay to the death," Sipar promised earnestly.

"Don't strain yourself," said Duncan.

He picked up the rifle and walked down to the waterhole.

The night was quiet and the land continued to have that empty feeling. Empty except for the fire and the waterhole and the little micelike animals running in the thicket.

And Sipar—Sipar lying by the fire, curled up and sound asleep already. Naked, with not a weapon to its hand—just the naked animal, the basic humanoid, and yet with underlying purpose that at times was baffling. Scared and shivering this morning at mere mention of the Cytha, yet never faltering on the trail; in pure funk back there on the knoll where they had lost the Cytha, but now ready to go on to the death.

Duncan went back to the fire and prodded Sipar with his toe. The native came straight up out of sleep.

"Whose death?" asked Duncan. "Whose death were you talking of?"

"Why, ours, of course," said Sipar, and went back to sleep.

III

Suncan did not see the arrow coming. He heard the swishing whistle and felt the wind of it on the right side of his throat and then it thunked into a tree behind him.

He leaped aside and dived for the cover of a tumbled mound of boulders and almost instinctively his thumb pushed the fire control of the rifle up to automatic.

He crouched behind the jumbled rocks and peered ahead. There was not a thing to see. The hula-trees shimmered in the blaze of sun and the thorn-bush was gray and lifeless and the only things astir were three stilt-birds walking gravely a quarter of a mile away.

"Sipar!" he whispered.

"Here, mister."

"Keep low. It's still out there."

Whatever it might be. Still out there and waiting for another shot. Duncan shivered, remembering the feel of the arrow flying past his throat. A hell of a way for a man to die—out at the tail-end of nowhere with an arrow in his throat and a scared-stiff native heading back for home as fast as it could go.

He flicked the control on the rifle back to single fire, crawled around the rock pile and sprinted for a grove of trees that stood on higher ground. He reached them, and there he flanked the spot from which the arrow must have come.

He unlimbered the binoculars and glassed the area. He still saw no sign. Whatever had taken the pot shot at them had made its getaway.

He walked back to the tree where the arrow still stood out, its point driven deep into the bark. He grasped the shaft and wrenched the arrow free.

"You can come out now," he called to Sipar. "There's no one around."

The arrow was unbelievably crude. The unfeathered shaft looked as if it had been battered off to the proper length with a jagged stone. The arrowhead was unflaked flint picked up from some outcropping or dry creek bed, and it was awkwardly bound to the shaft with the tough but pliant inner bark of the hula-tree.

"You recognize this?" he asked Sipar.

The native took the arrow and examined it. "Not my tribe."

"Of course not your tribe. Yours wouldn't take a shot at us. Some other tribe, perhaps?"

"Very poor arrow."

"I know that. But it could kill you just as dead as if it were a good one. Do you recognize it?"

"No tribe made this arrow," Sipar declared.

"Child, maybe?"

"What would child do way out here?"

"That's what I thought, too," said Duncan.

He took the arrow back, held it between his thumbs and forefingers, and twirled it slowly, with a terrifying thought nibbling at his brain. It couldn't be. It was too fantastic. He wondered if the sun was finally getting him that he had thought of it at all.

He squatted down and dug at the ground with the makeshift arrow point. "Sipar, what do you actually know about the Cytha?"

"Nothing, mister. Scared of it is all."

"We aren't turning back. If there's something that you know— something that would help us. . . ."

It was as close as he could come to begging aid. It was further than he had meant to go. He should not have asked at all, he thought angrily.

"I do not know," the native said.

Duncan cast the arrow to one side and rose to his feet. He cradled the rifle in his arm. "Let's go."

He watched Sipar trot ahead. Crafty little stinker, he told himself. It knows more than it's telling.

They toiled into the afternoon. It was, if possible, hotter and drier than the day before. There was a sense of tension in the air—no, that was rot. And even if there were, a man must act as if it were not there. If he let himself fall prey to every mood out in this empty land, he only had himself to blame for whatever happened to him.

The tracking was harder now. The day before, the Cytha had only run away, straight-line fleeing to keep ahead of them, to stay out of their reach. Now it was becoming tricky. It backtracked often in an attempt to throw them off. Twice in the afternoon, the trail blanked out entirely and it was only after long searching that Sipar picked it up again—in one instance, a mile away from where it had vanished in thin air.

That vanishing bothered Duncan more than he would admit. Trails do not disappear entirely, not when the terrain remains the same, not when the weather is unchanged. Something was going on, something, perhaps, that Sipar knew far more about than it was willing to divulge.

He watched the native closely, and there seemed nothing suspicious. It continued at its work. It was, for all to see, the good and faithful hound.

Late in the afternoon, the plain on which they had been traveling suddenly dropped away. They stood poised on the brink of a great escarpment and looked far out to great tangled forests and a flowing river.

It was like suddenly coming into another and beautiful room that one had not expected.

This was new land, never seen before by any Earthman. For no one had ever mentioned that somewhere to the west a forest lay beyond the bush. Men coming in from space had seen it, probably, but only as a different color-marking on the planet. To them, it made no difference.

But to the men who lived on Layard, to the planter and the trader, the prospector and the hunter, it was important. And I, thought Duncan with a sense of triumph, am the man who found it.

"Mister!"

"Now what?"

"Out there. *Skun!*"

"I don't—"

"Out there, mister. Across the river."

Duncan saw it then—a haze in the blueness of the rift—a puff of copper moving very fast, and as he watched, he heard the far-off keening of the storm, a shiver in the air rather than a sound.

He watched in fascination as it moved along the river and saw the boiling fury it made out of the forest. It struck and crossed the river, and the river for a moment seemed to stand on end, with a sheet of silvery water splashed toward the sky.

Then it was gone as quickly as it had happened, but there was a tumbled slash across the forest where the churning winds had traveled.

Back at the farm, Zikkara had warned him of the *skun*. This was the season for them, it had said, and a man caught in one wouldn't have a chance.

Duncan let his breath out slowly.

"Bad," said Sipar.

"Yes, very bad."

"Hit fast. No warning."

"What about the trail?" asked Duncan. "Did the Cytha—"

Sipar nodded downward.

"Can we make it before nightfall?"

"I think so," Sipar answered.

It was rougher than they had thought. Twice they went down blind trails that pinched off, with sheer rock faces opening out into drops of hundreds of feet, and were forced to climb again and find another way.

They reached the bottom of the escarpment as the brief twilight closed in, and they hurried to gather firewood. There was no water, but a little was still left in their canteens, and they made do with that.

After their scant meal of rockahominy, Sipar rolled himself into a ball and went to sleep immediately.

Duncan sat with his back against a boulder which one day, long ago, had fallen from the slope above them, but was now half buried in the soil that through the ages had kept sifting down.

Two days gone, he told himself.

Was there, after all, some truth in the whispered tales that made the rounds back at the settlements—that no one should waste his time in tracking down a Cytha, since a Cytha was unkillable?

Nonsense, he told himself. And yet the hunt had toughened, the trail become more difficult, the Cytha a much more cunning and elusive quarry. Where it had run from them the day before, now it fought to shake them off. And if it did that the second day, why had it not tried to throw them off the first? And what about the third day—tomorrow?

He shook his head. It seemed incredible that an animal would become more formidable as the hunt progressed. But that seemed to be exactly what had happened. More spooked, perhaps, more frightened—only the Cytha did not act like a frightened beast. It was acting like an animal that was gaining savvy and determination, and that was somehow frightening.

From far off to the west, toward the forest and the river, came the laughter and the howling of a pack of screamers. Duncan leaned his rifle against the boulder and got up to pile more wood on the fire. He stared out into the western darkness, listening to the racket. He made a wry face and pushed a hand absent-mindedly through his hair. He put out a silent hope that the screamers would decide to keep their distance. They were something a man could do without.

Behind him, a pebble came bumping down the slope. It thudded to a rest just short of the fire.

Duncan spun around. Foolish thing to do, he thought, to camp so near the slope. If something big should start to move, they'd be out of luck.

He stood and listened. The night was quiet. Even the screamers had shut up for the moment. Just one rolling rock and he had his hackles up. He'd have to get himself in hand.

He went back to the boulder, and as he stooped to pick up the rifle, he heard the faint beginning of a rumble. He straightened swiftly to face the scarp that blotted out the star-strewn sky—and the rumble grew!

In one leap, he was at Sipar's side. He reached down and grasped the native by an arm, jerked it erect, held it on its feet. Sipar's eyes snapped open, blinking in the firelight.

The rumble had grown to a roar, and there were thumping nois-es, as of heavy boulders bouncing, and beneath the roar the silky, ominous rustle of sliding soil and rock.

Sipar jerked its arm free of Duncan's grip and plunged into the darkness. Duncan whirled and followed.

They ran, stumbling in the dark, and behind them the roar of the sliding, bouncing rock became a throaty roll of thunder that filled the night from brim to brim. As he ran, Duncan could feel, in dread anticipation, the gusty breath of hurtling debris blowing on his neck, the crushing impact of a boulder smashing into him, the engulfing flood of tumbling talus snatching at his legs.

A puff of billowing dust came out and caught them and they ran choking as well as stumbling. Off to the left of them, a mighty chunk of rock chugged along the ground in jerky, almost reluctant fashion.

Then the thunder stopped and all one could hear was the small slitherings of the lesser debris as it trickled down the slope.

Duncan stopped running and slowly turned around. The camp-fire was gone, buried, no doubt, beneath tons of overlay, and the stars had paled because of the great cloud of dust which still bil-lowed up into the sky.

He heard Sipar moving near him and reached out a hand, searching for the tracker, not knowing exactly where it was. He found the native, grasped it by the shoulder and pulled it up beside him.

Sipar was shivering.

"It's all right," said Duncan.

And it *was* all right, he reassured himself. He still had the rifle. The extra drum of ammunition and the knife were on his belt, the bag of rockahominy in his pocket. The canteens were all they had lost—the canteens and the fire.

"We'll have to hole up somewhere for the night," Duncan said. "There are screamers on the loose."

He didn't like what he was thinking, nor the sharp edge of fear that was beginning to crowd in upon him. He tried to shrug it off, but it still stayed with him, just out of reach.

Sipar plucked at his elbow.

"Thorn thicket, mister. Over there. We could crawl inside. We would be safe from screamers."

It was torture, but they made it.

"Screamers and you are taboo," said Duncan, suddenly remembering. "How come you are afraid of them?"

"Afraid for you, mister, mostly. Afraid for myself just a little. Screamers could forget. They might not recognize me until too late. Safer here."

"I agree with you," said Duncan.

The screamers came and padded all about the thicket. The beasts sniffed and clawed at the thorns to reach them, but finally went away.

When morning came, Duncan and Sipar climbed the scarp, clambering over the boulders and the tons of soil and rock that covered their camping place. Following the gash cut by the slide, they clambered up the slope and finally reached the point of the slide's beginning.

There they found the depression in which the poised slab of rock had rested and where the supporting soil had been dug away so that it could be started, with a push, down the slope above the campfire.

And all about were the deeply sunken paw marks of the Cytha!

IV

Now it was more than just a hunt. It was knife against the throat, kill or be killed. Now there was no stopping, when before there might have been. It was no longer sport and there was no mercy.

"And that's the way I like it," Duncan told himself.

He rubbed his hand along the rifle barrel and saw the metallic glints shine in the noonday sun. One more shot, he prayed. Just give me one more shot at it. This time there will be no slip-up. This time there will be more than three sodden hunks of flesh and fur lying in the grass to mock me.

He squinted his eyes against the heat shimmer rising from the river, watching Sipar hunkered beside the water's edge.

The native rose to its feet and trotted back to him.

"It crossed," said Sipar. "It walked out as far as it could go and it must have swum."

"Are you sure? It might have waded out to make us think it crossed, then doubled back again."

He stared at the purple-green of the trees across the river. Inside that forest, it would be hellish going.

"We can look," said Sipar.

"Good. You go downstream. I'll go up."

An hour later, they were back. They had found no tracks. There seemed little doubt the Cytha had really crossed the river.

They stood side by side, looking at the forest.

"Mister, we have come far. You are brave to hunt the Cytha. You have no fear of death."

"The fear of death," Duncan said, "is entirely infantile. And it's beside the point as well. I do not intend to die."

They waded out into the stream. The bottom shelved gradually, and they had to swim no more than a hundred yards or so.

They reached the forest bank and threw themselves flat to rest. Duncan looked back the way that they had come. To the east, the escarpment was a dark-blue smudge against the pale-blue burnished sky. And two days back of that lay the farm and the *vua* field, but they seemed much farther off than that. They were lost in time and distance; they belonged to another existence and another world.

All his life, it seemed to him, had faded and become inconsequential and forgotten, as if this moment in his life were the only one that counted; as if all the minutes and the hours, all the breaths and heartbeats, wake and sleep, had pointed toward this certain hour upon this certain stream, with the rifle molded to his hand and the cool, calculated bloodlust of a killer riding in his brain.

Sipar finally got up and began to range along the stream. Duncan sat up and watched.

Scared to death, he thought, and yet it stayed with me. At the campfire that first night, it had said it would stick to the death and apparently it had meant exactly what it said. It's hard, he thought, to figure out these jokers, hard to know what kind of mental operation, what seethings of emotion, what brand of ethics and what variety of belief and faith go to make them and their way of life.

It would have been so easy for Sipar to have missed the trail and swear it could not find it. Even from the start, it could have refused to go. Yet, fearing, it had gone. Reluctant, it had trailed. Without any need for faithfulness and loyalty, it had been loyal and faithful. But loyal to what, Duncan wondered. To him, the outlander and intruder? Loyal to itself? Or perhaps, although that seemed impossible, faithful to the Cytha?

What does Sipar think of me, he asked himself, and maybe more to the point, what do I think of Sipar? Is there a common meeting ground? Or are we, despite our humanoid forms, condemned forever to be alien and apart?

He held the rifle across his knees and stroked it, polishing it, petting it, making it even more closely a part of him, an instrument of his deadliness, an expression of his determination to track and kill the Cytha.

Just another chance, he begged. Just one second, or even less, to draw a steady bead. That is all I want, all I need, all I'll ask.

Then he could go back across the days that he had left behind him, back to the farm and field, back into that misty other life from which he had been so mysteriously divorced, but which in time undoubtedly would become real and meaningful again.

Sipar came back. "I found the trail."

Duncan heaved himself to his feet. "Good."

They left the river and plunged into the forest, and there the heat closed in more mercilessly than ever—humid, stifling heat that felt like a soggy blanket wrapped tightly round the body.

The trail lay plain and clear. The Cytha now, it seemed, was intent upon piling up a lead without recourse to evasive tactics. Perhaps it had reasoned that its pursuers would lose some time at the river, and it may have been trying to stretch out that margin even further. Perhaps it needed that extra time, he speculated, to set up the necessary machinery for another dirty trick.

Sipar stopped and waited for Duncan to catch up. "Your knife, mister?"

Duncan hesitated. "What for?"

"I have a thorn in my foot," the native said. "I have to get it out."

Duncan pulled the knife from his belt and tossed it. Sipar caught it deftly.

Looking straight at Duncan, with the flicker of a smile upon its lips, the native cut its throat.

V

He should go back, he knew. Without the tracker, he didn't have a chance. The odds were now with the Cytha—if, indeed, they had not been with it from the very start.

Unkillable? Unkillable because it grew in intelligence to meet emergencies? Unkillable because, pressed, it could fashion a bow and arrow, however crude? Unkillable because it had a sense of tactics, like rolling rocks at night upon its enemy? Unkillable because a native tracker would cheerfully kill itself to protect the Cytha?

A sort of crisis-beast, perhaps? One able to develop intelligence and abilities to meet each new situation and then lapsing back to the level of non-intelligent contentment? That, thought Duncan, would be a sensible way for anything to live. It would do away with the inconvenience and the irritability and the discontentment of intelligence when intelligence was unneeded. But the intelligence, and the abilities which went with it, would be there, safely tucked away where one could reach in and get them, like a necklace or a gun—something to be used or to be put away as the case might be.

Duncan hunched forward and with a stick of wood pushed the fire together. The flames blazed up anew and sent sparks flying up into the whispering darkness of the trees. The night had cooled off a little, but the humidity still hung on and a man felt uncomfortable—a little frightened, too.

Duncan lifted his head and stared up into the fire-flecked darkness. There were no stars because the heavy foliage shut them out. He missed the stars. He'd feel better if he could look up and see them.

When morning came, he should go back. He should quit this hunt which now had become impossible and even slightly foolish.

But he knew he wouldn't. Somewhere along the three-day trail, he had become committed to a purpose and a challenge, and he knew that when morning came, he would go on again. It was not hatred that drove him, nor vengeance, nor even the trophy-urge—the hunter-lust that prodded men to kill something strange or harder to kill or bigger than any man had ever killed before. It was something more than that, some weird entangling of the Cytha's meaning with his own.

He reached out and picked up the rifle and laid it in his lap. Its barrel gleamed dully in the flickering campfire light, and he rubbed his hand along the stock as another man might stroke a woman's throat.

"Mister," said a voice.

It did not startle him, for the word was softly spoken, and for a moment he had forgotten that Sipar was dead—dead with a half-smile fixed upon its face and with its throat laid wide open.

"Mister?"

Duncan stiffened.

Sipar was dead and there was no one else—and yet someone had spoken to him, and there could be only one thing in all this wilderness that might speak to him.

"Yes," he said.

He did not move. He simply sat there, with the rifle in his lap.

"You know who I am?"

"I suppose you are the Cytha."

"You have done well," the Cytha said. "You've made a splendid hunt. There is no dishonor if you should decide to quit. Why don't you go back? I promise you no harm."

It was over there, somewhere in front of him, somewhere in the brush beyond the fire, almost straight across the fire from him, Duncan told himself. If he could keep it talking, perhaps even lure it out—

"Why should I?" he asked. "The hunt is never done until one gets the thing one is after."

"I can kill you," the Cytha told him. "But I do not want to kill. It hurts to kill."

"That's right," said Duncan. "You are most perceptive."

For he had it pegged now. He knew exactly where it was. He could afford a little mockery.

His thumb slid up the metal and nudged the fire control to automatic and he flexed his legs beneath him so that he could rise and fire in one single motion.

"Why did you hunt me?" the Cytha asked. "You are a stranger on my world, and you had no right to hunt me. Not that I mind, of course. In fact, I found it stimulating. We must do it again. When I am ready to be hunted, I shall come and tell you and we can spend a day or two at it."

"Sure we can," said Duncan, rising. And as he rose into his crouch, he held the trigger down and the gun danced in insane fury, the muzzle flare a flicking tongue of hatred and the hail of death hissing spitefully in the underbrush.

"Anytime you want to," yelled Duncan gleefully, "I'll come and hunt you! You just say the word, and I'll be on your tail. I might even kill you. How do you like it, chump!"

And he held the trigger tight and kept his crouch so the slugs would not fly high, but would cut their swath just above the ground, and he moved the muzzle back and forth a lot so that he covered extra ground to compensate for any miscalculations he might have made.

The magazine ran out and the gun clicked empty and the vicious chatter stopped. Powder smoke drifted softly in the campfire light and the smell of it was perfume in the nostrils and in the underbrush many little feet were running, as if a thousand frightened mice were scurrying from catastrophe.

Duncan unhooked the extra magazine from where it hung upon his belt and replaced the empty one. Then he snatched a burning length of wood from the fire and waved it frantically until it burst into a blaze and became a torch. Rifle grasped in one hand and the torch in the other, he plunged into the underbrush. Little chittering things fled to escape him.

He did not find the Cytha. He found chewed-up bushes and soil churned by flying metal, and he found five lumps of flesh and fur, and these he brought back to the fire.

Now the fear that had been stalking him, keeping just beyond his reach, walked out from the shadows and hunkered by the campfire with him.

He placed the rifle within easy reach and arranged the five bloody chunks on the ground close to the fire and he tried with trembling fingers to restore them to the shape they'd been before the bullets struck them. And that was a good one, he thought with grim irony, because they had no shape. They had been part of the Cytha and you killed a Cytha inch by inch, not with a single shot. You knocked a pound of meat off it the first time, and the next time you shot off another pound or two, and if you got enough shots at it, you finally carved it down to size and maybe you could kill it then, although he wasn't sure.

He was afraid. He admitted that he was and he squatted there and watched his fingers shake and he kept his jaws clamped tight to stop the chatter of his teeth.

The fear had been getting closer all the time; he knew it had moved in by a step or two when Sipar cut its throat, and why in the name of God had the damn fool done it? It made no sense at all. He had wondered about Sipar's loyalties, and the very loyalties that he had dismissed as a sheer impossibility had been the answer, after all. In the end, for some obscure reason—obscure to humans, that is—Sipar's loyalty had been to the Cytha.

But then what was the use of searching for any reason in it? Nothing that had happened made any sense. It made no sense that a beast one was pursuing should up and talk to one—although it did fit in with the theory of the crisis-beast he had fashioned in his mind.

Progressive adaptation, he told himself. Carry adaptation far enough and you'd reach communication. But might not the Cytha's power of adaptation be running down? Had the Cytha gone about as far as it could force itself to go? Maybe so, he thought. It might be worth a gamble. Sipar's suicide, for all its casualness, bore the overtones of last-notch desperation. And the Cytha's speaking to Duncan, its attempt to parley with him, contained a note of weakness.

The arrow had failed and the rockslide had failed and so had Sipar's death. What next would the Cytha try? Had it anything to try?

Tomorrow he'd find out. Tomorrow he'd go on. He couldn't turn back now.

He was too deeply involved. He'd always wonder, if he turned back now, whether another hour or two might not have seen the end of it. There were too many questions, too much mystery—there was now far more at stake than ten rows of *vua*.

Another day might make some sense of it, might banish the dread walker that trod upon his heels, might bring some peace of mind.

As it stood right at the moment, none of it made sense.

But even as he thought it, suddenly one of the bits of bloody flesh and mangled fur made sense.

Beneath the punching and prodding of his fingers, it had assumed a shape.

Breathlessly, Duncan bent above it, not believing, not even wanting to believe, hoping frantically that it should prove completely wrong.

But there was nothing wrong with it. The shape was there and could not be denied. It had somehow fitted back into its natural shape and it was a baby screamer—well, maybe not a baby, but at least a tiny screamer.

Duncan sat back on his heels and sweated. He wiped his bloody hands upon the ground. He wondered what other shapes he'd find if he put back into proper place the other hunks of limpness that lay beside the fire.

He tried and failed. They were too smashed and torn.

He picked them up and tossed them in the fire. He took up his rifle and walked around the fire, sat down with his back against a tree, cradling the gun across his knees.

Those little scurrying feet, he wondered—like the scampering of a thousand busy mice. He had heard them twice, that first night in the thicket by the waterhole and again tonight.

And what could the Cytha be? Certainly not the simple, uncomplicated, marauding animal he had thought to start with.

A hive-beast? A host animal? A thing masquerading in many different forms?

Shotwell, trained in such deductions, might make a fairly accurate guess, but Shotwell was not here. He was at the farm, fretting, more than likely, over Duncan's failure to return.

Finally the first light of morning began to filter through the forest, and it was not the glaring, clean white light of the open plain and bush, but a softened, diluted, fuzzy green light to match the smothering vegetation.

The night noises died away, and the noises of the day took up—the sawings of unseen insects, the screechings of hidden birds and something far away began to make a noise that sounded like an empty barrel falling slowly down a stairway.

What little coolness the night had brought dissipated swiftly and the heat clamped down, a breathless, relentless heat that quivered in the air.

Circling, Duncan picked up the Cytha trail not more than a hundred yards from camp.

The beast had been traveling fast. The pug marks were deeply sunk and widely spaced. Duncan followed as rapidly as he dared. It was a temptation to follow at a run, to match the Cytha's speed, for the trail was plain and fresh and it fairly beckoned.

And that was wrong, Duncan told himself. It was too fresh, too plain—almost as if the animal had gone to endless trouble so that the human could not miss the trail.

He stopped his trailing and crouched beside a tree and studied the tracks ahead. His hands were too tense upon the gun, his body keyed too high and fine. He forced himself to take slow, deep breaths. He had to calm himself. He had to loosen up.

He studied the tracks ahead—four bunched pug marks, then a long leap interval, then four more bunched tracks, and between the sets of marks the forest floor was innocent and smooth.

Too smooth, perhaps. Especially the third one from him. Too smooth and somehow artificial, as if someone had patted it with gentle hands to make it unsuspicious.

Duncan sucked his breath in slowly.

Trap?

Or was his imagination playing tricks on him?

And if it were a trap, he would have fallen into it if he had kept on following as he had started out.

Now there was something else, a strange uneasiness, and he stirred uncomfortably, casting frantically for some clue to what it was.

He rose and stepped out from the tree, with the gun at ready. What a perfect place to set a trap, he thought. One would be looking at the pug marks, never at the space between them, for the space between would be neutral ground, safe to stride out upon.

Oh, clever Cytha, he said to himself. Oh, clever, clever Cytha!

And now he knew what the other trouble was—the great uneasiness. It was the sense of being watched.

Somewhere up ahead, the Cytha was crouched, watching and waiting—anxious or exultant, maybe even with laughter rumbling in its throat.

He walked slowly forward until he reached the third set of tracks and he saw that he had been right. The little area ahead was smoother than it should be.

"Cytha!" he called.

His voice was far louder than he had meant it to be and he stood astonished and a bit abashed.

Then he realized why it was so loud.

It was the only sound there was!

The forest suddenly had fallen silent. The insects and birds were quiet and the thing in the distance had quit falling down the stairs. Even the leaves were silent. There was no rustle in them and they hung limp upon their stems.

There was a feeling of doom and the green light had changed to a copper light and everything was still.

And the light was *copper*!

Duncan spun around in panic. There was no place for him to hide.

Before he could take another step, the *skun* came and the winds rushed out of nowhere. The air was clogged with flying leaves and debris. Trees snapped and popped and tumbled in the air.

The wind hurled Duncan to his knees, and as he fought to regain his feet, he remembered, in a blinding flash of total recall, how it had looked from atop the escarpment—the boiling fury of the winds and the mad swirling of the coppery mist and how the trees had whipped in whirlpool fashion.

He came half erect and stumbled, clawing at the ground in an attempt to get up again, while inside his brain an insistent, clicking voice cried out for him to run, and somewhere another voice said to lie flat upon the ground, to dig in as best he could.

Something struck him from behind and he went down, pinned flat, with his rifle wedged beneath him. He cracked his head upon the ground and the world whirled sickeningly and plastered his face with a handful of mud and tattered leaves.

He tried to crawl and couldn't, for something had grabbed him by the ankle and was hanging on.

With a frantic hand, he clawed the mess out of his eyes, spat it from his mouth.

Across the spinning ground, something black and angular tumbled rapidly. It was coming straight toward him and he saw it was the Cytha and that in another second it would be on top of him.

He threw up an arm across his face, with the elbow crooked, to take the impact of the wind-blown Cytha and to ward it off.

But it never reached him. Less than a yard away, the ground opened up to take the Cytha and it was no longer there.

Suddenly the wind cut off and the leaves once more hung motionless and the heat clamped down again and that was the end of it. The *skun* had come and struck and gone.

Minutes, Duncan wondered, or perhaps no more than seconds. But in those seconds, the forest had been flattened and the trees lay in shattered heaps.

He raised himself on an elbow and looked to see what was the matter with his foot and he saw that a fallen tree had trapped his foot beneath it.

He tugged a few times experimentally. It was no use. Two close-set limbs, branching almost at right angles from the hole, had been driven deep into the ground and his foot, he saw, had been caught at the ankle in the fork of the buried branches.

The foot didn't hurt—not yet. It didn't seem to be there at all. He tried wiggling his toes and felt none.

He wiped the sweat off his face with a shirt sleeve and fought to force down the panic that was rising in him. Getting panicky was the worst thing a man could do in a spot like this. The thing to do was to take stock of the situation, figure out the best approach, then go ahead and try it.

The tree looked heavy, but perhaps he could handle it if he had to, although there was the danger that if he shifted it, the bole might settle more solidly and crush his foot beneath it. At the moment, the two heavy branches, thrust into the ground on either side of his ankle, were holding most of the tree's weight off his foot.

The best thing to do, he decided, was to dig the ground away beneath his foot until he could pull it out.

He twisted around and started digging with the fingers of one hand. Beneath the thin covering of humus, he struck a solid surface and his fingers slid along it.

With mounting alarm, he explored the ground, scratching at the humus. There was nothing but rock—some long-buried boulder, the top of which lay just beneath the ground.

His foot was trapped beneath a heavy tree and a massive boulder, held securely in place by forked branches that had forced their splintering way down along the boulder's sides.

He lay back, propped on an elbow. It was evident that he could do nothing about the buried boulder. If he was going to do anything, his problem was the tree.

To move the tree, he would need a lever, and he had a good, stout lever in his rifle. It would be a shame, he thought a little wryly, to use a gun for such a purpose, but he had no choice.

He worked for an hour, and it was no good. Even with the rifle as a pry, he could not budge the tree.

He lay back, defeated, breathing hard, wringing wet with perspiration.

He grimaced at the sky.

All right, Cytha, he thought, you won out in the end. But it took a *skun* to do it. With all your tricks, you couldn't do the job until. . . .

Then he remembered.

He sat up hurriedly.

"Cytha!" he called.

The Cytha had fallen into a hole that had opened in the ground. The hole was less than an arm's length away from him, with a little debris around its edges still trickling into it.

Duncan stretched out his body, lying flat upon the ground, and looked into the hole. There, at the bottom of it, was the Cytha.

It was the first time he'd gotten a good look at the Cytha, and it was a crazily put-together thing. It seemed to have nothing functional about it, and it looked more like a heap of something, just thrown on the ground, than it did an animal.

The hole, he saw, was more than an ordinary hole. It was a pit and very cleverly constructed. The mouth was about four feet in diameter, and it widened to roughly twice that at the bottom. It was, in general, bottle-shaped, with an incurving shoulder at the top so that anything that fell in could not climb out. Anything falling into that pit was in to stay.

This, Duncan knew, was what had lain beneath that too-smooth interval between the two sets of Cytha tracks. The Cytha had worked all night to dig it, then had carried away the dirt dug out of the pit and had built a flimsy camouflage cover over it. Then it had gone back and made the trail that was so loud and clear, so easy to make out and follow. And having done all that, having labored hard and stealthily, the Cytha had settled down to watch, to make sure the following human had fallen in the pit.

"Hi, pal," said Duncan. "How are you making out?"

The Cytha did not answer.

"Classy pit," said Duncan. "Do you always den up in luxury like this?"

But the Cytha didn't answer.

Something queer was happening to the Cytha. It was coming all apart.

Duncan watched with fascinated horror as the Cytha broke down into a thousand lumps of motion that scurried in the pit and tried to scramble up its sides, only to fall back in tiny showers of sand.

Amid the scurrying lumps, one thing remained intact, a fragile object that resembled nothing quite so much as the stripped skeleton of a Thanksgiving turkey. But it was a most extraordinary Thanksgiving skeleton, for it throbbed with pulsing life and glowed with a steady violet light.

Chitterings and squeakings came out of the pit, and the soft patter of tiny running feet, and as Duncan's eyes became accustomed to the darkness of the pit, he began to make out the forms of some of the scurrying shapes. There were tiny screamers and some donovans and sawmill birds and a bevy of kill-devils and something else as well.

Duncan raised a hand and pressed it against his eyes, then took it quickly away. The little faces still were there, looking up as if beseeching him, with the white shine of their teeth and the white rolling of their eyes.

He felt horror wrenching at his stomach, and the sour, bitter taste of revulsion welled into his throat, but he fought it down, harking back to that day at the farm before they had started on the hunt.

"I can track down anything but screamers, stilt-birds, long-horns and donovans," Sipar had told him solemnly. "These are my taboos."

And Sipar was also their taboo, for he had not feared the donovan. Sipar had been, however, somewhat fearful of the screamers in the dead of night because, the native had told him reasonably, screamers were forgetful.

Forgetful of what? Forgetful of the Cytha-mother? Forgetful of the motley brood in which they had spent their childhood?

For that was the only answer to what was running in the pit and the whole, unsuspected answer to the enigma against which men like Shotwell had frustratedly banged their heads for years.

Strange, he told himself. All right, it might be strange, but if it worked, what difference did it make? So the planet's denizens were sexless because there was no need of sex—what was wrong with that? It might, in fact, Duncan admitted to himself, head off a lot of trouble. No family spats, no triangle trouble, no fighting over mates. While it might be unexciting, it did seem downright peaceful.

And since there was no sex, the Cytha species was the planetary mother—but more than just a mother. The Cytha, more than likely, was mother-father, incubator, nursery, teacher and perhaps many other things besides, all rolled into one.

In many ways, he thought, it might make a lot of sense. Here natural selection would be ruled out and ecology could be controlled in considerable degree, and mutation might even be a matter of deliberate choice rather than random happenstance.

And it would make for a potential planetary unity such as no other world had ever known. Everything here was kin to everything else. Here was a planet where Man, or any other alien, must learn to tread most softly. For it was not inconceivable that, in a crisis or a clash of interests, one might find himself faced suddenly with a unified and cooperating planet, with every form of life making common cause against the interloper.

The little scurrying things had given up; they'd gone back to their places, clustered around the pulsing violet of the Thanksgiving skeleton, each one fitting into place until the Cytha had taken shape again. As if, Duncan told himself, blood and nerve and muscle had come back from a brief vacation to form the beast anew.

"Mister," asked the Cytha, "what do we do now?"

"You should know," Duncan told it. "You were the one who dug the pit."

"I split myself," the Cytha said. "A part of me dug the pit and the other part that stayed on the surface got me out when the job was done."

"Convenient," grunted Duncan.

And it *was* convenient. That was what had happened to the Cytha when he had shot at it—it had split into all its component parts and had got away. And that night beside the waterhole, it had spied on him, again in the form of all its separate parts, from the safety of the thicket.

"You are caught and so am **I**," the Cytha said. "Both of us will die here. It seems a fitting end to our association. Do you not agree with me?"

"I'll get you out," said Duncan wearily. "I have no quarrel with children."

He dragged the rifle toward him and unhooked the sling from the stock. Carefully he lowered the gun by the sling, still attached to the barrel, down into the pit.

The Cytha reared up and grasped it with its forepaws.

"Easy now," Duncan cautioned. "You're heavy. I don't know if I can hold you."

But he needn't have worried. The little ones were detaching themselves and scrambling up the rifle and the sling. They reached his extended arms and ran up them with scrabbling claws. Little sneering screamers and the comic stilt-birds and the mouse-size kill-devils that snarled at him as they climbed. And the little grinning natives—not babies, scarcely children, but small editions of full-grown humanoids. And the weird donovans scampering happily.

They came climbing up his arms and across his shoulders and milled about on the ground beside him, waiting for the others.

And finally the Cytha, not skinned down to the bare bones of its Thanksgiving-turkey-size, but far smaller than it had been, climbed awkwardly up the rifle and the sling to safety.

Duncan hauled the rifle up and twisted himself into a sitting position.

The Cytha, he saw, was reassembling.

He watched in fascination as the restless miniatures of the planet's life swarmed and seethed like a hive of bees, each one clicking into place to form the entire beast.

And now the Cytha was complete. Yet small—still small—no more than lion-size.

"But it is such a little one," Zikkara had argued with him that morning at the farm. "It is such a young one."

Just a young brood, no more than suckling infants—if suckling was the word, or even some kind of wild approximation. And through the months and years, the Cytha would grow, with the growing of its diverse children, until it became a monstrous thing.

It stood there looking at Duncan and the tree.

"Now," said Duncan, "if you'll push on the tree, I think that between the two of us—"

"It is too bad," the Cytha said, and wheeled itself about.

He watched it go loping off.

"Hey!" he yelled.

But it didn't stop.

He grabbed up the rifle and had it halfway to his shoulder before he remembered how absolutely futile it was to shoot at the Cytha.

He let the rifle down.

"The dirty, ungrateful, double-crossing—"

He stopped himself. There was no profit in rage. When you were in a jam, you did the best you could. You figured out the problem and you picked the course that seemed best and you didn't panic at the odds.

He laid the rifle in his lap and started to hook up the sling and it was not till then that he saw the barrel was packed with sand and dirt.

He sat numbly for a moment, thinking back to how close he had been to firing at the Cytha, and if that barrel was packed hard enough or deep enough, he might have had an exploding weapon in his hands.

He had used the rifle as a crowbar, which was no way to use a gun. That was one way, he told himself, that was guaranteed to ruin it.

Duncan hunted around and found a twig and dug at the clogged muzzle, but the dirt was jammed too firmly in it and he made little progress.

He dropped the twig and was hunting for another stronger one when he caught the motion in a nearby clump of brush.

He watched closely for a moment and there was nothing, so he resumed the hunt for a stronger twig. He found one and started poking at the muzzle and there was another flash of motion.

He twisted around. Not more than twenty feet away, a screamer sat easily on its haunches. Its tongue was lolling out, and it had what looked like a grin upon its face.

And there was another, just at the edge of the clump of brush where he had caught the motion first.

There were others as well, he knew. He could hear them sliding through the tangle of fallen trees, could sense the soft padding of their feet.

The executioners, he thought.

The Cytha certainly had not wasted any time.

He raised the rifle and rapped the barrel smartly on the fallen tree, trying to dislodge the obstruction in the bore. But it didn't budge; the barrel still was packed with sand.

But no matter—he'd have to fire anyhow and take whatever chance there was.

He shoved the control to automatic and tilted up the muzzle.

There were six of them now, sitting in a ragged row, grinning at him, not in any hurry. They were sure of him, and there was no hurry. He'd still be there when they decided to move in.

And there were others—on all sides of him.

Once it started, he wouldn't have a chance.

"It'll be expensive, gents," he told them.

And he was astonished at how calm, how coldly objective he could be, now that the chips were down. But that was the way it was, he realized.

He'd thought, a while ago, how a man might suddenly find himself face to face with an aroused and cooperating planet. Maybe this was it in miniature.

The Cytha had obviously passed the word along: *Man back there needs killing. Go and get him.*

Just like that, for a Cytha would be the power here. A life force, the giver of life, the decider of life, the repository of all animal life on the entire planet.

There was more than one of them, of course. Probably they had home districts, spheres of influence and responsibility mapped out. And each one would be a power supreme in its own district.

Momism, he thought with a sour grin. Momism at its absolute peak.

Nevertheless, he told himself, it wasn't too bad a system if you wanted to consider it objectively.

But he was in a poor position to be objective about that or anything else.

The screamers were inching closer, hitching themselves forward slowly on their bottoms.

"I'm going to set up a deadline for you critters," Duncan called out. "Just two feet farther, up to that rock, and I let you have it."

He'd get all six of them, of course, but the shots would be the signal for the general rush by all those other animals slinking in the brush.

If he were free, if he were on his feet, possibly he could beat them off. But pinned as he was, he didn't have a chance. It would be all over less than a minute after he opened fire. He might, he figured, last as long as that.

The six inched closer and he raised the rifle.

But they stopped and moved no farther. Their ears lifted just a little, as if they might be listening, and the grins dropped from their faces. They squirmed uneasily and assumed a look of guilt and, like shadows, they were gone, melting away so swiftly that he scarcely saw them go.

Duncan sat quietly, listening, but he could hear no sound.

Reprieve, he thought. But for how long? Something had scared them off, but in a while they might be back. He had to get out of here, and he had to make it fast.

If he could find a longer lever, he could move the tree. There was a branch slanting up from the topside of the fallen tree. It was almost four inches at the butt and it carried its diameter well.

He slid the knife from his belt and looked at it. Too small, too thin, he thought, to chisel through a four-inch branch, but it was all he had. When a man was desperate enough, though, when his very life depended on it, he would do anything.

He hitched himself along, sliding toward the point where the branch protruded from the tree. His pinned leg protested with stabs of pain as his body wrenched it around. He gritted his teeth and pushed himself closer. Pain slashed through his leg again, and he was still long inches from the branch.

He tried once more, then gave up. He lay panting on the ground.

There was just one thing left.

He'd have to try to hack out a notch in the trunk just above his leg. No, that would be next to impossible, for he'd be cutting into the whorled and twisted grain at the base of the supporting fork.

Either that or cut off his foot, and that was even more impossible. A man would faint before he got the job done.

It was useless, he knew. He could do neither one. There was nothing he could do.

For the first time, he admitted it to himself: He would stay here and die. Shotwell, back at the farm, in a day or two might set out hunting for him. But Shotwell would never find him. And anyhow, by nightfall, if not sooner, the screamers would be back.

He laughed gruffly in his throat—laughing at himself.

The Cytha had won the hunt hands down. It had used a human weakness to win and then had used that same human weakness to achieve a viciously poetic vengeance.

After all, what could one expect? One could not equate human ethics with the ethics of the Cytha. Might not human ethics, in certain cases, seem as weird and illogical, as infamous and ungrateful, to an alien?

He hunted for a twig and began working again to clean the rifle bore.

A crashing behind him twisted him around and he saw the Cytha. Behind the Cytha stalked a donovan.

He tossed away the twig and raised the gun.

"No," said the Cytha sharply.

The donovan tramped purposefully forward and Duncan felt the prickling of the skin along his back. It was a frightful thing. Nothing could stand before a donovan. The screamers had turned tail and run when they had heard it a couple of miles or more away.

The donovan was named for the first known human to be killed by one. That first was only one of many. The roll of donovan-victims ran long, and no wonder, Duncan thought. It was the closest he had ever been to one of the beasts, and he felt a coldness creeping over him. It was like an elephant and a tiger and a grizzly bear wrapped in the selfsame hide. It was the most vicious fighting machine that ever had been spawned.

He lowered the rifle. There would be no point in shooting. In two quick strides, the beast could be upon him.

The donovan almost stepped on him, and he flinched away. Then the great head lowered and gave the fallen tree a butt, and the tree bounced for a yard or two. The donovan kept on walking. Its powerfully muscled stern moved into the brush and out of sight.

"Now we are even," said the Cytha. "I had to get some help."

Duncan grunted. He flexed the leg that had been trapped and he could not feel the foot. Using his rifle as a cane, he pulled himself erect. He tried putting weight on the injured foot and it screamed with pain.

He braced himself with the rifle and rotated so that he faced the Cytha.

"Thanks, pal," he said. "I didn't think you'd do it."

"You will not hunt me now?"

Duncan shook his head. "I'm in no shape for hunting. I am heading home."

"It was the *vua*, wasn't it? That was why you hunted me?"

"The *vua* is my livelihood," said Duncan. "I cannot let you eat it."

The Cytha stood silently, and Duncan watched it for a moment. Then he wheeled. Using the rifle for a crutch, he started hobbling away.

The Cytha hurried to catch up with him.

"Let us make a bargain, mister. I will not eat the *vua* and you will not hunt me. Is that fair enough?"

"That is fine with me," said Duncan. "Let us shake on it."

He put down a hand and the Cytha lifted up a paw. They shook, somewhat awkwardly, but very solemnly.

"Now," the Cytha said, "I will see you home. The screamers would have you before you got out of the woods."

VI

They halted on a knoll. Below them lay the farm, with the *vua* rows straight and green in the red soil of the fields.

"You can make it from here," the Cytha said. "I am wearing thin. It is an awful effort to keep on being smart. I want to go back to ignorance and comfort."

"It was nice knowing you," Duncan told it politely. "And thanks for sticking with me."

He started down the hill, leaning heavily on the rifle-crutch. Then he frowned troubledly and turned back.

"Look," he said, "you'll go back to animal again. Then you will forget. One of these days, you'll see all that nice, tender *vua* and—"

"Very simple," said the Cytha. "If you find me in the *vua*, just begin hunting me. With you after me, I will quickly get smart and remember once again, and it will be all right."

"Sure," agreed Duncan. "I guess that will work."

The Cytha watched him go stumping down the hill.

Admirable, it thought. Next time I have a brood, I think I'll raise a dozen like him.

It turned around and headed for the deeper brush.

It felt intelligence slipping from it, felt the old, uncaring comfort coming back again. But it glowed with anticipation, seethed with happiness at the big surprise it had in store for its new-found friend.

Won't he be happy and surprised when I drop them at his door, it thought.

Will he be ever pleased!

THE STREET THAT WASN'T THERE

Mr. Jonathon Chambers left his house on Maple Street at exactly seven o'clock in the evening and set out on the daily walk he had taken, at the same time, come rain or snow, for twenty solid years.

The walk never varied. He paced two blocks down Maple Street, stopped at the Red Star confectionery to buy a Rose Trofero perfecto, then walked to the end of the fourth block on Maple. There he turned right on Lexington, followed Lexington to Oak, down Oak and so by way of Lincoln back to Maple again and to his home.

He didn't walk fast. He took his time. He always returned to his front door at exactly 7:45. No one ever stopped to talk with him. Even the man at the Red Star confectionery, where he bought his cigar, remained silent while the purchase was being made. Mr. Chambers merely tapped on the glass top of the counter with a coin, the man reached in and brought forth the box, and Mr. Chambers took his cigar. That was all.

For people long ago had gathered that Mr. Chambers desired to be left alone. The newer generation of townsfolk called it eccentricity. Certain uncouth persons had a different word for it. The oldsters remembered that this queer looking individual with his black silk muffler, rosewood cane and bowler hat once had been a professor at State University.

A professor of metaphysics, they seemed to recall, or some such outlandish subject. At any rate a furore of some sort was connected with his name . . . at the time an academic scandal. He had written a book, and he had taught the subject matter of that volume to his classes. What that subject matter was, had long been forgotten, but whatever it was had been considered sufficiently revolutionary to cost Mr. Chambers his post at the university.

A silver moon shone over the chimney tops and a chill, impish October wind was rustling the dead leaves when Mr. Chambers started out at seven o'clock.

It was a good night, he told himself, smelling the clean, crisp air of autumn and the faint pungence of distant wood smoke.

He walked unhurriedly, swinging his cane a bit less jauntily than twenty years ago. He tucked the muffler more securely under the rusty old topcoat and pulled his bowler hat more firmly on his head.

He noticed that the street light at the corner of Maple and Jefferson was out and he grumbled a little to himself when he was forced to step off the walk to circle a boarded-off section of newly-laid concrete work before the driveway of 816.

It seemed that he reached the corner of Lexington and Maple just a bit too quickly, but he told himself that this couldn't be. For he never did that. For twenty years, since the year following his expulsion from the university, he had lived by the clock.

The same thing, at the same time, day after day. He had not deliberately set upon such a life of routine. A bachelor, living alone with sufficient money to supply his humble needs, the timed existence had grown on him gradually.

So he turned on Lexington and back on Oak. The dog at the corner of Oak and Jefferson was waiting for him once again and came out snarling and growling, snapping at his heels. But Mr. Chambers pretended not to notice and the beast gave up the chase.

A radio was blaring down the street and faint wisps of what it was blurting floated to Mr. Chambers.

". . . still taking place . . . Empire State building disappeared . . . thin air . . . famed scientist, Dr. Edmund Harcourt. . . ."

The wind whipped the muted words away and Mr. Chambers grumbled to himself. Another one of those fantastic radio dramas, probably. He remembered one from many years before, something about the Martians. And Harcourt! What did Harcourt have to do with it? He was one of the men who had ridiculed the book Mr. Chambers had written.

But he pushed speculation away, sniffed the clean, crisp air again, looked at the familiar things that materialized out of the late autumn darkness as he walked along. For there was nothing . . . absolutely nothing in the world . . . that he would let upset him. That was a tenet he had laid down twenty years ago.

There was a crowd of men in front of the drugstore at the corner of Oak and Lincoln and they were talking excitedly. Mr. Chambers caught some excited words: "It's happening everywhere. . . . What do you think it is. . . . The scientists can't explain. . . ."

But as Mr. Chambers neared them they fell into what seemed an abashed silence and watched him pass. He, on his part, gave them no sign of recognition. That was the way it had been for many years, ever since the people had become convinced that he did not wish to talk.

One of the men half started forward as if to speak to him, but then stepped back and Mr. Chambers continued on his walk.

Back at his own front door he stopped and as he had done a thousand times before drew forth the heavy gold watch from his pocket.

He started violently. It was only 7:30!

For long minutes he stood there staring at the watch in accusation. The timepiece hadn't stopped, for it still ticked audibly.

But 15 minutes too soon! For twenty years, day in, day out, he had started out at seven and returned at a quarter of eight. Now. . . .

It wasn't until then that he realized something else was wrong. He had no cigar. For the first time he had neglected to purchase his evening smoke.

Shaken, muttering to himself, Mr. Chambers let himself in his house and locked the door behind him.

He hung his hat and coat on the rack in the hall and walked slowly into the living room. Dropping into his favorite chair, he shook his head in bewilderment.

Silence filled the room. A silence that was measured by the ticking of the old fashioned pendulum clock on the mantelpiece.

But silence was no strange thing to Mr. Chambers. Once he had loved music . . . the kind of music he could get by tuning in symphonic orchestras on the radio. But the radio stood silent in the corner, the cord out of its socket. Mr. Chambers had pulled it out many years before. To be precise, upon the night when the symphonic broadcast had been interrupted to give a news flash.

He had stopped reading newspapers and magazines too, had exiled himself to a few city blocks. And as the years flowed by, that self exile had become a prison, an intangible, impassable wall bounded by four city blocks by three. Beyond them lay utter, unexplainable terror. Beyond them he never went.

But recluse though he was, he could not on occasion escape from hearing things. Things the newsboy shouted on the streets, things the men talked about on the drugstore corner when they didn't see him coming.

And so he knew that this was the year 1960 and that the wars in Europe and Asia had flamed to an end to be followed by a terrible plague, a plague that even now was sweeping through country after country like wild fire, decimating populations. A plague undoubtedly induced by hunger and privation and the miseries of war.

But those things he put away as items far removed from his own small world. He disregarded them. He pretended he had never heard of them. Others might discuss and worry over them if they wished. To him they simply did not matter.

But there were two things tonight that did matter. Two curious, incredible events. He had arrived home fifteen minutes early. He had forgotten his cigar.

Huddled in the chair, he frowned slowly. It was disquieting to have something like that happen. There must be something wrong. Had his long exile finally turned his mind . . . perhaps just a very little . . . enough to make him queer? Had he lost his sense of proportion, of perspective?

No, he hadn't. Take this room, for example. After twenty years it had come to be as much a part of him as the clothes he wore. Every detail of the room was engraved in his mind with . . . clarity; the old center leg table with its green covering and stained glass lamp; the mantelpiece with the dusty bric-a-brac; the pendulum clock that told the time of day as well as the day of the week and month; the elephant ash tray on the tabaret and, most important of all, the marine print.

Mr. Chambers loved that picture. It had depth, he always said. It showed an old sailing ship in the foreground on a placid sea. Far in the distance, almost on the horizon line, was the vague outline of a larger vessel.

There were other pictures, too. The forest scene above the fireplace, the old English prints in the corner where he sat, the Currier and Ives above the radio. But the ship print was directly in his line of vision. He could see it without turning his head. He had put it there because he liked it best.

Further reverie became an effort as Mr. Chambers felt himself succumbing to weariness. He undressed and went to bed. For an hour he lay awake, assailed by vague fears he could neither define nor understand.

When finally he dozed off it was to lose himself in a series of horrific dreams. He dreamed first that he was a castaway on a tiny islet in mid-ocean, that the waters around the island teemed with huge poisonous sea snakes . . . hydrophinnae . . . and that steadily those serpents were devouring the island.

In another dream he was pursued by a horror which he could neither see nor hear, but only could imagine. And as he sought to flee he stayed in the one place. His legs worked frantically, pumping like pistons, but he could make no progress. It was as if he ran upon a treadway.

Then again the terror descended on him, a black, unimagined thing and he tried to scream and couldn't. He opened his mouth and strained his vocal cords and filled his lungs to bursting with the urge to shriek . . . but not a sound came from his lips.

All next day he was uneasy and as he left the house that evening, at precisely seven o'clock, he kept saying to himself: "You must not forget tonight! You must remember to stop and get your cigar!"

The street light at the corner of Jefferson was still out and in front of 816 the cemented driveway was still boarded off. Everything was the same as the night before.

And now, he told himself, the Red Star confectionery is in the next block. I must not forget tonight. To forget twice in a row would be just too much.

He grasped that thought firmly in his mind, strode just a bit more rapidly down the street.

But at the corner he stopped in consternation. Bewildered, he stared down the next block. There was no neon sign, no splash of friendly light upon the sidewalk to mark the little store tucked away in this residential section.

He stared at the street marker and read the word slowly: GRANT. He read it again, unbelieving, for this shouldn't be Grant Street, but Marshall. He had walked two blocks and the confectionery was between Marshall and Grant. He hadn't come to Marshall yet . . . and here was Grant.

Or had he, absent-mindedly, come one block farther than he thought, passed the store as on the night before?

For the first time in twenty years, Mr. Chambers retraced his steps. He walked back to Jefferson, then turned around and went back to Grant again and on to Lexington. Then back to Grant again, where he stood astounded while a single, incredible fact grew slowly in his brain:

There wasn't any confectionery! The block from Marshall to Grant had disappeared!

Now he understood why he had missed the store on the night before, why he had arrived home fifteen minutes early.

On legs that were dead things he stumbled back to his home. He slammed and locked the door behind him and made his way unsteadily to his chair in the corner.

What was this? What did it mean? By what inconceivable necromancy could a paved street with houses, trees and buildings be spirited away and the space it had occupied be closed up?

Was something happening in the world which he, in his secluded life, knew nothing about?

Mr. Chambers shivered, reached to turn up the collar of his coat, then stopped as he realized the room must be warm. A fire blazed merrily in the grate. The cold he felt came from something . . . somewhere else. The cold of fear and horror, the chill of a half whispered thought.

A deathly silence had fallen, a silence still measured by the pendulum clock. And yet a silence that held a different tenor than he had ever sensed before. Not a homey, comfortable silence . . . but a silence that hinted at emptiness and nothingness.

There was something back of this, Mr. Chambers told himself. Something that reached far back into one corner of his brain and demanded recognition. Something tied up with the fragments of talk he had heard on the drugstore corner, bits of news broadcasts he had heard as he walked along the street, the shrieking of the newsboy calling his papers. Something to do with the happenings in the world from which he had excluded himself.

He brought them back to mind now and lingered over the one central theme of the talk he overheard: the wars and plagues. Hints of a Europe and Asia swept almost clean of human life, of the plague ravaging Africa, of its appearance in South America, of the frantic efforts of the United States to prevent its spread into that nation's boundaries.

Millions of people were dead in Europe and Asia, Africa and South America. Billions, perhaps.

And somehow those gruesome statistics seemed tied up with his own experience. Something, somewhere, some part of his earlier life, seemed to hold an explanation. But try as he would his befuddled brain failed to find the answer.

The pendulum clock struck slowly, its every other chime as usual setting up a sympathetic vibration in the pewter vase that stood upon the mantel.

Mr. Chambers got to his feet, strode to the door, opened it and looked out.

Moonlight tesselated the street in black and silver, etching the chimneys and trees against a silvered sky.

But the house directly across the street was not the same. It was strangely lop-sided, its dimensions out of proportion, like a house that suddenly had gone mad.

He stared at it in amazement, trying to determine what was wrong with it. He recalled how it had always stood, foursquare, a solid piece of mid-Victorian architecture.

Then, before his eyes, the house righted itself again. Slowly it drew together, ironed out its queer angles, readjusted its dimensions, became once again the stodgy house he knew it had to be.

With a sigh of relief, Mr. Chambers turned back into the hall.

But before he closed the door, he looked again. The house was lop-sided . . . as bad, perhaps worse than before!

Gulping in fright, Mr. Chambers slammed the door shut, locked it and double bolted it. Then he went to his bedroom and took two sleeping powders.

His dreams that night were the same as on the night before. Again there was the islet in mid-ocean. Again he was alone upon it. Again the squirming hydrophinnae were eating his foothold piece by piece.

He awoke, body drenched with perspiration. Vague light of early dawn filtered through the window. The clock on the bedside table showed 7:30. For a long time he lay there motionless.

Again the fantastic happenings of the night before came back to haunt him and as he lay there, staring at the windows, he remembered them, one by one. But his mind, still fogged by sleep and astonishment, took the happenings in its stride, mulled over them, lost the keen edge of fantastic terror that lurked around them.

The light through the windows slowly grew brighter. Mr. Chambers slid out of bed, slowly crossed to the window, the cold of the floor biting into his bare feet. He forced himself to look out.

There was nothing outside the window. No shadows. As if there might be a fog. But no fog, however, thick, could hide the apple tree that grew close against the house.

But the tree was there . . . shadowy, indistinct in the gray, with a few withered apples still clinging to its boughs, a few shriveled leaves reluctant to leave the parent branch.

The tree was there now. But it hadn't been when he first had looked. Mr. Chambers was sure of that.

And now he saw the faint outlines of his neighbor's house . . . but those outlines were all wrong. They didn't jibe and fit together . . . they were out of plumb. As if some giant hand had grasped the house and wrenched it out of true. Like the house he had seen across the street the night before, the house that had painfully righted itself when he thought of how it should look.

Perhaps if he thought of how his neighbor's house should look, it too might right itself. But Mr. Chambers was very weary. Too weary to think about the house.

He turned from the window and dressed slowly. In the living room he slumped into his chair, put his feet on the old cracked ottoman. For a long time he sat, trying to think.

And then, abruptly, something like an electric shock ran through him. Rigid, he sat there, limp inside at the thought. Minutes later he arose and almost ran across the room to the old mahogany bookcase that stood against the wall.

There were many volumes in the case: his beloved classics on the first shelf, his many scientific works on the lower shelves. The second shelf contained but one book. And it was around this book that Mr. Chambers' entire life was centered.

Twenty years ago he had written it and foolishly attempted to teach its philosophy to a class of undergraduates. The newspapers, he remembered, had made a great deal of it at the time. Tongues had been set to wagging. Narrow-minded townsfolk, failing to understand either his philosophy or his aim, but seeing in him another exponent of some anti-rational cult, had forced his expulsion from the school.

It was a simple book, really, dismissed by most authorities as merely the vagaries of an over-zealous mind.

Mr. Chambers took it down now, opened its cover and began thumbing slowly through the pages. For a moment the memory of happier days swept over him.

Then his eyes focused on the paragraph, a paragraph written so long ago the very words seemed strange and unreal:

Man himself, by the power of mass suggestion, holds the physical fate of this earth . . . yes, even the universe. Billions of minds seeing trees as trees, houses as houses, streets as streets . . . and not as something else. Minds that see things as they are and have kept things as they were. . . . Destroy those minds and the entire foundation of matter, robbed of its regenerative power, will crumple and slip away like a column of sand. . . .

His eyes followed down the page:

Yet this would have nothing to do with matter itself . . . but only with matter's form. For while the mind of man through long ages may have moulded an imagery of that space in which he lives, mind would have little conceivable influence upon the existence of that matter. What exists in our known universe shall exist always and can never be destroyed, only altered or transformed.

But in modern astrophysics and mathematics we gain an insight into the possibility . . . yes probability . . . that there are other dimensions, other brackets of time and space impinging on the one we occupy.

If a pin is thrust into a shadow, would that shadow have any knowledge of the pin? It would not, for in this case the shadow is two dimensional, the pin three dimensional. Yet both occupy the same space.

Granting then that the power of men's minds alone holds this universe, or at least this world in its present form, may we not go farther and envision other minds in some other plane watching us, waiting, waiting craftily for the time they can take over the domination of matter? Such a concept is not impossible. It is a natural conclusion if we accept the double hypothesis: that mind does control the formation of all matter; and that other worlds lie in juxtaposition with ours.

Perhaps we shall come upon a day, far distant, when our plane, our world will dissolve beneath our feet and before our eyes as some stronger intelligence reaches out from the dimensional shadows of the very space we live in and wrests from us the matter which we know to be our own.

He stood astounded beside the bookcase, his eyes staring unseeing into the fire upon the hearth.

He had written that. And because of those words he had been called a heretic, had been compelled to resign his position at the university, had been forced into this hermit life.

A tumultuous idea hammered at him. Men had died by the millions all over the world. Where there had been thousands of minds there now were one or two. A feeble force to hold the form of matter intact.

The plague had swept Europe and Asia almost clean of life, had blighted Africa, had reached South America . . . might even have come to the United States. He remembered the whispers he had heard, the words of the men at the drugstore corner, the buildings disappearing. Something scientists could not explain. But those were merely scraps of information. He did not know the whole story . . . he could not know. He never listened to the radio, never read a newspaper.

But abruptly the whole thing fitted together in his brain like the missing piece of a puzzle into its slot. The significance of it all gripped him with damning clarity.

There were not sufficient minds in existence to retain the material world in its mundane form. Some other power from another dimension was fighting to supersede man's control *and take his universe into its own plane!*

Abruptly Mr. Chambers closed the book, shoved it back in the case and picked up his hat and coat.

He had to know more. He had to find someone who could tell him.

He moved through the hall to the door, emerged into the street. On the walk he looked skyward, trying to make out the sun. But there wasn't any sun . . . only an all pervading grayness that shrouded everything . . . not a gray fog, but a gray emptiness that seemed devoid of life, of any movement.

The walk led to his gate and there it ended, but as he moved forward the sidewalk came into view and the house ahead loomed out of the gray, but a house with differences.

He moved forward rapidly. Visibility extended only a few feet and as he approached them the houses materialized like two dimensional pictures without perspective, like twisted cardboard soldiers lining up for review on a misty morning.

Once he stopped and looked back and saw that the grayness had closed in behind him. The houses were wiped out, the sidewalk faded into nothing.

He shouted, hoping to attract attention. But his voice frightened him. It seemed to ricochet up and into the higher levels of the sky, as if a giant door had been opened to a mighty room high above him.

He went on until he came to the corner of Lexington. There, on the curb, he stopped and stared. The gray wall was thicker there but he did not realize how close it was until he glanced down at his feet and saw there was nothing, nothing at all beyond the curbstone. No dull gleam of wet asphalt, no sign of a street. It was as if all eternity ended here at the corner of Maple and Lexington.

With a wild cry, Mr. Chambers turned and ran. Back down the street he raced, coat streaming after him in the wind, bowler hat bouncing on his head.

Panting, he reached the gate and stumbled up the walk, thankful that it still was there.

On the stoop he stood for a moment, breathing hard. He glanced back over his shoulder and a queer feeling of inner numbness seemed to well over him. At that moment the gray nothingness appeared to thin . . . the enveloping curtain fell away, and he saw. . . .

Vague and indistinct, yet cast in stereoscopic outline, a gigantic city was lined against the darkling sky. It was a city fantastic with cubed domes, spires, and aerial bridges and flying buttresses. Tunnel-like streets, flanked on either side by shining metallic ramps and runways, stretched endlessly to the vanishing point. Great shafts of multicolored light probed huge streamers and ellipses above the higher levels.

And beyond, like a final backdrop, rose a titanic wall. It was from that wall . . . from its crenelated parapets and battlements that Mr. Chambers felt the eyes peering at him.

Thousands of eyes glaring down with but a single purpose.

And as he continued to look, something else seemed to take form above that wall. A design this time, that swirled and writhed in the ribbons of radiance and rapidly coalesced into strange geometric features, without definite line or detail. A colossal face, a face of indescribable power and evil, it was, staring down with malevolent composure.

Then the city and the face slid out of focus; the vision faded like a darkened magic-lantern, and the grayness moved in again.

Mr. Chambers pushed open the door of his house. But he did not lock it. There was no need of locks . . . not any more.

A few coals of fire still smouldered in the grate and going there, he stirred them up, raked away the ash, piled on more wood. The flames leaped merrily, dancing in the chimney's throat.

Without removing his hat and coat, he sank exhausted in his favorite chair, closed his eyes then opened them again.

He sighed with relief as he saw the room was unchanged. Everything in its accustomed place: the clock, the lamp, the elephant ash tray, the marine print on the wall.

Everything was as it should be. The clock measured the silence with its measured ticking; it chimed abruptly and the vase sent up its usual sympathetic vibration.

This was his room, he thought. Rooms acquire the personality of the person who lives in them, become a part of him. This was his world, his own private world, and as such it would be the last to go.

But how long could he . . . his brain . . . maintain its existence?

Mr. Chambers stared at the marine print and for a moment a little breath of reassurance returned to him. *They* couldn't take this away. The rest of the world might dissolve because there was insufficient power of thought to retain its outward form.

But this room was his. He alone had furnished it. He alone, since he had first planned the house's building, had lived here.

This room would stay. It must stay on . . . it must. . . .

He rose from his chair and walked across the room to the book case, stood staring at the second shelf with its single volume. His eyes shifted to the top shelf and swift terror gripped him.

For all the books weren't there. A lot of books weren't there! Only the most beloved, the most familiar ones.

So the change already had started here! The unfamiliar books were gone and that fitted in the pattern . . . for it would be the least familiar things that would go first.

Wheeling, he stared across the room. Was it his imagination, or did the lamp on the table blur and begin to fade away?

But as he stared at it, it became clear again, a solid, substantial thing.

For a moment real fear reached out and touched him with chilly fingers. For he knew that this room no longer was proof against the thing that had happened out there on the street.

Or had it really happened? Might not all this exist within his own mind? Might not the street be as it always was, with laughing children and barking dogs? Might not the Red Star confectionery still exist, splashing the street with the red of its neon sign?

Could it be that he was going mad? He had heard whispers when he had passed, whispers the gossiping housewives had not intended him to hear. And he had heard the shouting of boys when he walked by. They thought him mad. Could he be really mad?

But he knew he wasn't mad. He knew that he perhaps was the sanest of all men who walked the earth. For he, and he alone, had foreseen this very thing. And the others had scoffed at him for it.

Somewhere else the children might be playing on a street. But it would be a different street. And the children undoubtedly would be different too.

For the matter of which the street and everything upon it had been formed would now be cast in a different mold, stolen by different minds in a different dimension.

Perhaps we shall come upon a day, far distant, when our plane, our world will dissolve beneath our feet and before our eyes as some stronger intelligence reaches out from the dimensional shadows of the very space we live in and wrests from us the matter which we know to be our own.

But there had been no need to wait for that distant day. Scant years after he had written those prophetic words the thing was happening. Man had played unwittingly into the hands of those other minds in the other dimension. Man had waged a war and war had bred a pestilence. And the whole vast cycle of events was but a detail of a cyclopean plan.

He could see it all now. By an insidious mass hypnosis minions from that other dimension . . . or was it one supreme intelligence . . . had deliberately sown the seeds of dissension. The reduction of the world's mental power had been carefully planned with dia-bolic premeditation.

On impulse he suddenly turned, crossed the room and opened the connecting door to the bedroom. He stopped on the threshold and a sob forced its way to his lips.

There was no bedroom. Where his stolid four poster and dress-er had been there was greyish nothingness.

Like an automaton he turned again and paced to the hall door. Here, too, he found what he had expected. There was no hall, no familiar hat rack and umbrella stand.

Nothing. . . .

Weakly Mr. Chambers moved back to his chair in the corner.

"So here I am," he said, half aloud.

So there he was. Embattled in the last corner of the world that was left to him.

Perhaps there were other men like him, he thought. Men who stood at bay against the emptiness that marked the transition from one dimension to another. Men who had lived close to the things they loved, who had endowed those things with such substan-tial form by power of mind alone that they now stood out alone against the power of some greater mind.

The street was gone. The rest of his house was gone. This room still retained its form.

This room, he knew, would stay the longest. And when the rest of the room was gone, this corner with his favorite chair would remain. For this was the spot where he had lived for twenty years. The bedroom was for sleeping, the kitchen for eating. This room was for living. This was his last stand.

These were the walls and floors and prints and lamps that had soaked up his will to make them walls and prints and lamps.

He looked out the window into a blank world. His neighbors' houses already were gone. They had not lived with them as he had lived with this room. Their interests had been divided, thinly spread; their thoughts had not been concentrated as his upon an area four blocks by three, or a room fourteen by twelve.

Staring through the window, he saw it again. The same vision he had looked upon before and yet different in an indescribable way. There was the city illumined in the sky. There were the elliptical towers and turrets, the cube-shaped domes and battlements. He could see with stereoscopic clarity the aerial bridges, the gleaming avenues sweeping on into infinitude. The vision was nearer this time, but the depth and proportion had changed . . . as if he were viewing it from two concentric angles at the same time.

And the face . . . the face of magnitude . . . of power of cosmic craft and evil. . . .

Mr. Chambers turned his eyes back into the room. The clock was ticking slowly, steadily. The greyness was stealing into the room.

The table and radio were the first to go. They simply faded away and with them went one corner of the room.

And then the elephant ash tray.

"Oh, well," said Mr. Chambers, "I never did like that very well."

Now as he sat there it didn't seem queer to be without the table or the radio. It was as if it were something quite normal. Something one could expect to happen.

Perhaps, if he thought hard enough, he could bring them back.

But, after all, what was the use? One man, alone, could not stand off the irresistible march of nothingness. One man, all alone, simply couldn't do it.

He wondered what the elephant ash tray looked like in that other dimension. It certainly wouldn't be an elephant ash tray nor would the radio be a radio, for perhaps they didn't have ash trays or radios or elephants in the invading dimension.

He wondered, as a matter of fact, what he himself would look like when he finally slipped into the unknown. For he was matter, too, just as the ash tray and radio were matter.

He wondered if he would retain his individuality . . . if he still would be a person. Or would he merely be a thing?

There was one answer to all of that. He simply didn't know.

Nothingness advanced upon him, ate its way across the room, stalking him as he sat in the chair underneath the lamp. And he waited for it.

The room, or what was left of it, plunged into dreadful silence.

Mr. Chambers started. The clock had stopped. Funny . . . the first time in twenty years.

He leaped from his chair and then sat down again.

The clock hadn't stopped.

It wasn't there.

There was a tingling sensation in his feet.

HELLHOUNDS OF THE COSMOS

The paper had gone to press, graphically describing the latest of the many horrible events which had been enacted upon the Earth in the last six months. The headlines screamed that Six Corners, a little hamlet in Pennsylvania, had been wiped out by the Horror. Another front-page story told of a Terror in the Amazon Valley which had sent the natives down the river in babbling fear. Other stories told of deaths here and there, all attributable to the "Black Horror," as it was called.

The telephone rang.

"Hello," said the editor.

"London calling," came the voice of the operator.

"All right," replied the editor.

He recognized the voice of Terry Masters, special correspondent. His voice came clearly over the transatlantic telephone.

"The Horror is attacking London in force," he said. "There are thousands of them and they have completely surrounded the city. All roads are blocked. The government declared the city under martial rule a quarter of an hour ago and efforts are being made to prepare for resistance against the enemy."

"Just a second," the editor shouted into the transmitter.

He touched a button on his desk, and in a moment an answering buzz told him he was in communication with the press-room.

"Stop the presses!" he yelled into the speaking tube. "Get ready for a new front make-up!"

"O.K.," came faintly through the tube, and the editor turned back to the phone.

"Now let's have it," he said, and the voice at the London end of the wire droned on, telling the story that in another half hour was read by a world which shuddered in cold fear even as it scanned the glaring headlines.

* * * *

"Woods," said the editor of the *Press* to a reporter, "run over and talk to Dr. Silas White. He phoned me to send someone. Something about this Horror business."

Henry Woods rose from his chair without a word and walked from the office. As he passed the wire machine it was tapping out, with a maddeningly methodical slowness, the story of the fall of London. Only half an hour before it had rapped forth the flashes concerning the attack on Paris and Berlin.

He passed out of the building into a street that was swarming with terrified humanity. Six months of terror, of numerous mysterious deaths, of villages blotted out, had set the world on edge. Now with London in possession of the Horror and Paris and Berlin fighting hopelessly for their lives, the entire population of the world was half insane with fright.

Exhorters on street corners enlarged upon the end of the world, asking that the people prepare for eternity, attributing the Horror to the act of a Supreme Being enraged with the wickedness of the Earth.

Expecting every moment an attack by the Horror, people left their work and gathered in the streets. Traffic, in places, had been blocked for hours and law and order were practically paralyzed. Commerce and transportation were disrupted as fright-ridden people fled from the larger cities, seeking doubtful hiding places in rural districts from the death that stalked the land.

A loudspeaker in front of a music store blared forth the latest news flashes.

"It has been learned," came the measured tones of the announcer, "that all communication with Berlin ceased about ten minutes ago. At Paris all efforts to hold the Horror at bay have been futile. Explosives blow it apart, but have the same effect upon it as explosion has on gas. It flies apart and then reforms again, not always in the same shape as it was before. A new gas, one of the most deadly ever conceived by man, has failed to have any effect on the things. Electric guns and heat guns have absolutely no effect upon them.

"A news flash which has just come in from Rome says that a large number of the Horrors has been sighted north of that city by airmen. It seems they are attacking the capitals of the world first. Word comes from Washington that every known form of defense is being amassed at that city. New York is also preparing. . . ."

Henry Woods fought his way through the crowd which milled in front of the loudspeaker. The hum of excitement was giving away to a silence, the silence of a stunned people, the fearful silence of a populace facing a presence it is unable to understand, an embattled world standing with useless weapons before an incomprehensible enemy.

In despair the reporter looked about for a taxi, but realized, with a groan of resignation, that no taxi could possibly operate in that crowded street. A street car, blocked by the stream of humanity which jostled and elbowed about it, stood still, a defeated thing.

Seemingly the only man with a definite purpose in that whirlpool of terror-stricken men and women, the newspaperman settled down to the serious business of battling his way through the swarming street.

"Before I go to the crux of the matter," said Dr. Silas White, about half an hour later, "let us first review what we know of this so-called Horror. Suppose you tell me exactly what you know of it."

Henry Woods shifted uneasily in his chair. Why didn't the old fool get down to business? The chief would raise hell if this story didn't make the regular edition. He stole a glance at his wristwatch. There was still almost an hour left. Maybe he could manage it. If the old chap would only snap into it!

"I know no more," he said, "than is common knowledge."

The gimlet eyes of the old white-haired scientist regarded the newspaperman sharply.

"And that is?" he questioned.

There was no way out of it, thought Henry. He'd have to humor the old fellow.

"The Horror," he replied, "appeared on Earth, so far as the knowledge of man is concerned, about six months ago."

Dr. White nodded approvingly.

"You state the facts very aptly," he said.

"How so?"

"When you say 'so far as the knowledge of man is concerned.'"

"Why is that?"

"You will understand in due time. Please proceed."

Vaguely the newspaperman wondered whether he was interviewing the scientist or the scientist interviewing him.

"They were first reported," Woods said, "early this spring. At that time they wiped out a small village in the province of Quebec. All the inhabitants, except a few fugitives, were found dead, killed mysteriously and half eaten, as if by wild beasts. The fugitives were demented, babbling of black shapes that swept down out of the dark forest upon the little town in the small hours of the morning.

"The next that was heard of them was about a week later, when they struck in an isolated rural district in Poland, killing and feeding on the population of several farms. In the next week more villages were wiped out, in practically every country on the face of the Earth. From the hinterlands came tales of murder done at midnight, of men and women horribly mangled, of livestock slaughtered, of buildings crushed as if by some titanic force.

"At first they worked only at night and then, seeming to become bolder and more numerous, attacked in broad daylight."

The newspaperman paused.

"Is that what you want?" he asked.

"That's part of it," replied Dr. White, "but that's not all. What do these Horrors look like?"

"That's more difficult," said Henry. "They have been reported as every conceivable sort of monstrosity. Some are large and others are small. Some take the form of animals, others of birds and reptiles, and some are cast in appalling shapes such as might be snatched out of the horrid imagery of a thing which resided in a world entirely alien to our own."

Dr. White rose from his chair and strode across the room to confront the other.

"Young man," he asked, "do you think it possible the Horror might have come out of a world entirely alien to our own?"

"I don't know," replied Henry. "I know that some of the scientists believe they came from some other planet, perhaps even from some other solar system. I know they are like nothing ever known before on Earth. They are always inky black, something like black tar, you know, sort of sticky-looking, a disgusting sight. The weapons of mankind can't affect them. Explosives are useless and so are projectiles. They wade through poison gas and fiery chemicals and seem to enjoy them. Elaborate electrical barriers have failed. Heat doesn't make them turn a hair."

"And you think they came from some other planet, perhaps some other solar system?"

"I don't know what to think," said Henry. "If they came out of space they must have come in some conveyance, and that would certainly have been sighted, picked up long before it arrived, by our astronomers. If they came in small conveyances, there must have been many of them. If they came in a single conveyance, it would be too large to escape detection. That is, unless—"

"Unless what?" snapped the scientist.

"Unless it traveled at the speed of light. Then it would have been invisible."

"Not only invisible," snorted the old man, "but non-existent."

A question was on the tip of the newspaperman's tongue, but before it could be asked the old man was speaking again, asking a question:

"Can you imagine a fourth dimension?"

"No, I can't," said Henry.

"Can you imagine a thing of only two dimensions?"

"Vaguely, yes."

The scientist smote his palms together.

"Now we're coming to it!" he exclaimed.

Henry Woods regarded the other narrowly. The old man must be turned. What did fourth and second dimensions have to do with the Horror?

"Do you know anything about evolution?" questioned the old man.

"I have a slight understanding of it. It is the process of upward growth, the stairs by which simple organisms climb to become more complex organisms."

Dr. White grunted and asked still another question:

"Do you know anything about the theory of the exploding universe? Have you ever noted the tendency of the perfectly balanced to run amuck?"

The reporter rose slowly to his feet.

"Dr. White," he said, "you phoned my paper you had a story for us. I came here to get it, but all you have done is ask me questions. If you can't tell me what you want us to publish, I will say good-day."

The doctor put forth a hand that shook slightly.

"Sit down, young man," he said. "I don't blame you for being impatient, but I will now come to my point."

The newspaperman sat down again.

"I have developed a hypothesis," said Dr. White, "and have conducted several experiments which seem to bear it out. I am staking my reputation upon the supposition that it is correct. Not only that, but I am also staking the lives of several brave men who believe implicitly in me and my theory. After all, I suppose it makes little difference, for if I fail the world is doomed, if I succeed it is saved from complete destruction.

"Have you ever thought that our evolutionists might be wrong, that evolution might be downward instead of upward? The theory of the exploding universe, the belief that all of creation is running down, being thrown off balance by the loss of energy, spurred onward by cosmic accidents which tend to disturb its equilibrium, to a time when it will run wild and space will be filled with swirling dust of disintegrated worlds, would bear out this contention.

"This does not apply to the human race. There is no question that our evolution is upward, that we have arisen from one-celled creatures wallowing in the slime of primal seas. Our case is probably paralleled by thousands of other intelligences on far-flung planets and island universes. These instances, however, running at cross purposes to the general evolutional trend of the entire cosmos, are mere flashes in the eventual course of cosmic evolution, comparing no more to eternity than a split second does to a million years.

"Taking these instances, then, as inconsequential, let us say that the trend of cosmic evolution is downward rather than upward, from complex units to simpler units rather than from simple units to more complex ones.

"Let us say that life and intelligence have degenerated. How would you say such a degeneration would take place? In just what way would it be manifested? What sort of transition would life pass through in passing from one stage to a lower one? Just what would be the nature of these stages?"

The scientist's eyes glowed brightly as he bent forward in his chair. The newspaperman said simply: "I have no idea."

"Man," cried the old man, "can't you see that it would be a matter of dimensions? From the fourth dimension to the third, from the third to the second, from the second to the first, from the first to a questionable existence or plane which is beyond our understanding or perhaps to oblivion and the end of life. Might not the fourth have evolved from a fifth, the fifth from a sixth, the sixth from a seventh, and so on to no one knows what multidimension?"

Dr. White paused to allow the other man to grasp the importance of his statements. Woods failed lamentably to do so.

"But what has this to do with the Horror?" he asked.

"Have you absolutely no imagination?" shouted the old man.

"Why, I suppose I have, but I seem to fail to understand."

"We are facing an invasion of fourth-dimensional creatures," the old man whispered, almost as if fearful to speak the words aloud. "We are being attacked by life which is one dimension above us in evolution. We are fighting, I tell you, a tribe of hellhounds out of the cosmos. They are unthinkably above us in the matter of intelligence. There is a chasm of knowledge between us so wide and so deep that it staggers the imagination. They regard us as mere animals, perhaps not even that. So far as they are concerned we are just fodder, something to be eaten as we eat vegetables and cereals or the flesh of domesticated animals. Perhaps they have watched us for years, watching life on the world increase, lapping their monstrous jowls over the fattening of the Earth. They have awaited the proper setting of the banquet table and now they are dining.

"Their thoughts are not our thoughts, their ideals not our ideals. Perhaps they have nothing in common with us except the primal basis of all life, self-preservation, the necessity of feeding.

"Maybe they have come of their own will. I prefer to believe that they have. Perhaps they are merely following the natural course of events, obeying some immutable law legislated by some higher being who watches over the cosmos and dictates what shall be and what shall not be. If this is true it means that there has been a flaw in my reasoning, for I believed that the life of each plane degenerated in company with the degeneration of its plane of existence, which would obey the same evolutional laws which govern the life upon it. I am quite satisfied that this invasion is a well-planned campaign, that some fourth-dimensional race has found a means of breaking through the veil of force which separates its plane from ours."

"But," pointed out Henry Woods, "you say they are fourth-dimensional things. I can't see anything about them to suggest an additional dimension. They are plainly three-dimensional."

"Of course they are three-dimensional. They would have to be to live in this world of three dimensions. The only two-dimensional objects which we know of in this world are merely illusions, projections of the third dimension, like a shadow. It is impossible for more than one dimension to live on any single plane.

"To attack us they would have to lose one dimension. This they have evidently done. You can see how utterly ridiculous it would be for you to try to attack a two-dimensional thing. So far as you were concerned it would have no mass. The same is true of the other dimensions. Similarly a being of a lesser plane could not harm an inhabitant of a higher plane. It is apparent that while the Horror has lost one material dimension, it has retained certain fourth-dimensional properties which make it invulnerable to the forces at the command of our plane."

The newspaperman was now sitting on the edge of his chair.

"But," he asked breathlessly, "it all sounds so hopeless. What can be done about it?"

Dr. White hitched his chair closer and his fingers closed with a fierce grasp upon the other's knee. A militant boom came into his voice.

"My boy," he said, "we are to strike back. We are going to invade the fourth-dimensional plane of these hellhounds. We are going to make them feel our strength. We are going to strike back."

Henry Woods sprang to his feet.

"How?" he shouted. "Have you . . . ?"

Dr. White nodded.

"I have found a way to send the third-dimensional into the fourth. Come and I will show you."

The machine was huge, but it had an appearance of simple construction. A large rectangular block of what appeared to be a strange black metal was set on end and flanked on each side by two smaller ones. On the top of the large block was set a half-globe of a strange substance, somewhat, Henry thought, like frosted glass. On one side of the large cube was set a lever, a long glass panel, two vertical tubes and three clock-face indicators. The control board, it appeared, was relatively simple.

Beside the mass of the five rectangles, on the floor, was a large plate of transparent substance, ground to a concave surface, through which one could see an intricate tangle of wire mesh.

Hanging from the ceiling, directly above the one on the floor, was another concave disk, but this one had a far more pronounced curvature.

Wires connected the two disks and each in turn was connected to the rectangular machine.

"It is a matter of the proper utilization of two forces, electrical and gravitational," proudly explained Dr. White. "Those two forces, properly used, warp the third-dimensional into the fourth. A reverse process is used to return the object to the third. The principle of the machine is—"

The old man was about to launch into a lengthy discussion, but Henry interrupted him. A glance at his watch had shown him press time was drawing perilously close.

"Just a second," he said. "You propose to warp a third-dimensional being into a fourth dimension. How can a third-dimensional thing exist there? You said a short time ago that only a specified dimension could exist on one single plane."

"You have missed my point," snapped Dr. White. "I am not sending a third-dimensional thing to a fourth dimension. I am changing the third-dimensional being into a fourth-dimensional being. I add a dimension, and automatically the being exists on a different plane. I am reversing evolution. This third dimension we now exist on evolved, millions of eons ago, from a fourth dimension. I am sending a lesser entity back over those millions of eons to a plane similar to one upon which his ancestors lived inconceivably long ago."

"But, man, how do you know you can do it?"

The doctor's eyes gleamed and his fingers reached out to press a bell.

A servant appeared almost at once.

"Bring me a dog," snapped the old man. The servant disappeared.

"Young man," said Dr. White, "I am going to show you how I know I can do it. I have done it before, now I am going to do it for you. I have sent dogs and cats back to the fourth dimension and returned them safely to this room. I can do the same with men."

The servant reappeared, carrying in his arms a small dog. The doctor stepped to the control board of his strange machine.

"All right, George," he said.

The servant had evidently worked with the old man enough to know what was expected of him. He stepped close to the floor disk and waited. The dog whined softly, sensing that all was not exactly right.

The old scientist slowly shoved the lever toward the right, and as he did so a faint hum filled the room, rising to a stupendous roar as he advanced the lever. From both floor disk and upper disk leaped strange cones of blue light, which met midway to form an hour-glass shape of brilliance.

The light did not waver or sparkle. It did not glow. It seemed hard and brittle, like straight bars of force. The newspaperman, gazing with awe upon it, felt that terrific force was there. What had the old man said? Warp a third-dimensional being into another dimension! That would take force!

As he watched, petrified by the spectacle, the servant stepped forward and, with a flip, tossed the little dog into the blue light. The animal could be discerned for a moment through the light and then it disappeared.

"Look in the globe!" shouted the old man; and Henry jerked his eyes from the column of light to the half-globe atop the machine.

He gasped. In the globe, deep within its milky center, glowed a picture that made his brain reel as he looked upon it. It was a scene such as no man could have imagined unaided. It was a horribly distorted projection of an eccentric landscape, a landscape hardly analogous to anything on Earth.

"That's the fourth dimension, sir," said the servant.

"That's not the fourth dimension," the old man corrected him. "That's a third-dimensional impression of the fourth dimension. It is no more the fourth dimension than a shadow is three-dimensional. It, like a shadow, is merely a projection. It gives us a glimpse of what the fourth plane is like. It is a shadow of that plane."

Slowly a dark blotch began to grow in the landscape. Slowly it assumed definite form. It puzzled the reporter. It looked familiar. He could have sworn he had seen it somewhere before. It was alive, for it had moved.

"That, sir, is the dog," George volunteered.

"That was the dog," Dr. White again corrected him. "God knows what it is now."

He turned to the newspaperman.

"Have you seen enough?" he demanded.

Henry nodded.

The other slowly began to return the lever to its original position. The roaring subsided, the light faded, the projection in the half-globe grew fainter.

"How are you going to use it?" asked the newspaperman.

"I have ninety-eight men who have agreed to be projected into the fourth dimension to seek out the entities that are attacking us and attack them in turn. I shall send them out in an hour."

"Where is there a phone?" asked the newspaperman.

"In the next room," replied Dr. White.

As the reporter dashed out of the door, the light faded entirely from between the two disks and on the lower one a little dog crouched, quivering, softly whimpering.

The old man stepped from the controls and approached the disk. He scooped the little animal from where it lay into his arms and patted the silky head.

"Good dog," he murmured; and the creature snuggled close to him, comforted, already forgetting that horrible place from which it had just returned.

"Is everything ready, George?" asked the old man.

"Yes, sir," replied the servant. "The men are all ready, even anxious to go. If you ask me, sir, they are a tough lot."

"They are as brave a group of men as ever graced the Earth," replied the scientist gently. "They are adventurers, every one of whom has faced danger and will not shrink from it. They are born fighters. My one regret is that I have not been able to secure more like them. A thousand men such as they should be able to conquer any opponent. It was impossible. The others were poor soft fools. They laughed in my face. They thought I was an old fool—I, the man who alone stands between them and utter destruction."

His voice had risen to almost a scream, but it again sank to a normal tone.

"I may be sending ninety-eight brave men to instant death. I hope not."

"You can always jerk them back, sir," suggested George.

"Maybe I can, maybe not," murmured the old man.

Henry Woods appeared in the doorway.

"When do we start?" he asked.

"We?" exclaimed the scientist.

"Certainly, you don't believe you're going to leave me out of this. Why, man, it's the greatest story of all time. I'm going as special war correspondent."

"They believed it? They are going to publish it?" cried the old man, clutching at the newspaperman's sleeve.

"Well, the editor was skeptical at first, but after I swore on all sorts of oaths it was true, he ate it up. Maybe you think that story didn't stop the presses!"

"I didn't expect them to. I just took a chance. I thought they, too, would laugh at me."

"But when do we start?" persisted Henry.

"You are really in earnest? You really want to go?" asked the old man, unbelievingly.

"I am going. Try to stop me."

Dr. White glanced at his watch.

"We will start in exactly thirty-four minutes," he said.

"Ten seconds to go." George, standing with watch in hand, spoke in a precise manner, the very crispness of his words betraying the excitement under which he labored.

The blue light, hissing, drove from disk to disk; the room thundered with the roar of the machine, before which stood Dr. White, his hand on the lever, his eyes glued on the instruments before him.

In a line stood the men who were to fling themselves into the light to be warped into another dimension, there to seek out and fight an unknown enemy. The line was headed by a tall man with hands like hams, with a weather-beaten face and a wild mop of hair. Behind him stood a belligerent little cockney. Henry Woods stood fifth in line. They were a motley lot, adventurers every one of them, and some were obviously afraid as they stood before that column of light, with only a few seconds of the third dimension left to them. They had answered a weird advertisement, and had but a limited idea of what they were about to do. Grimly, though, they accepted it as a job, a bizarre job, but a job. They faced it as they had faced other equally dangerous, but less unusual, jobs.

"Five seconds," snapped George.

The lever was all the way over now. The half-globe showed, within its milky interior, a hideously distorted landscape. The light had taken on a hard, brittle appearance and its hiss had risen to a scream. The machine thundered steadily with a suggestion of horrible power.

"Time up!"

The tall man stepped forward. His foot reached the disk; another step and he was bathed in the light, a third and he glimmered momentarily, then vanished. Close on his heels followed the little cockney.

With his nerves at almost a snapping point, Henry moved on behind the fourth man. He was horribly afraid, he wanted to break from the line and run, it didn't matter where, any place to get away from that steady, steely light in front of him. He had seen three men step into it, glow for a second, and then disappear. A fourth man had placed his foot on the disk.

Cold sweat stood out on his brow. Like an automaton he placed one foot on the disk. The fourth man had already disappeared.

"Snap into it, pal," growled the man behind.

Henry lifted the other foot, caught his toe on the edge of the disk and stumbled headlong into the column of light.

He was conscious of intense heat which was instantly followed by equally intense cold. For a moment his body seemed to be under enormous pressure, then it seemed to be expanding, flying apart, bursting, exploding. . . .

He felt solid ground under his feet, and his eyes, snapping open, saw an alien land. It was a land of somber color, with great gray moors, and beetling black cliffs. There was something queer about it, an intangible quality that baffled him.

He looked about him, expecting to see his companions. He saw no one. He was absolutely alone in that desolate brooding land. Something dreadful had happened! Was he the only one to be safely transported from the third dimension? Had some horrible accident occurred? Was he alone?

Sudden panic seized him. If something had happened, if the others were not here, might it not be possible that the machine would not be able to bring him back to his own dimension? Was he doomed to remain marooned forever in this terrible plane?

He looked down at his body and gasped in dismay. It was not his body!

It was a grotesque caricature of a body, a horrible profane mass of flesh, like a phantasmagoric beast snatched from the dreams of a lunatic.

It was real, however. He felt it with his hands, but they were not hands. They were something like hands; they served the same purpose that hands served in the third dimension. He was, he realized, a being of the fourth dimension, but in his fourth-dimensional brain still clung hard-fighting remnants of that faithful old third-dimensional brain. He could not, as yet, see with fourth-dimensional eyes, think purely fourth-dimensional thoughts. He had not oriented himself as yet to this new plane of existence. He was seeing the fourth dimension through the blurred lenses of millions of eons of third-dimensional existence. He was seeing it much more clearly than he had seen it in the half-globe atop the machine in Dr. White's laboratory, but he would not see it clearly until every vestige of the third dimension was wiped from him. That, he knew, would come in time.

He felt his weird body with those things that served as hands, and he found, beneath his groping, unearthly fingers, great rolling muscles, powerful tendons, and hard, well-conditioned flesh. A sense of well-being surged through him and he growled like an animal, like an animal of that horrible fourth plane.

But the terrible sounds that came from between his slobbering lips were not those of his own voice, they were the voices of many men.

Then he knew. He was not alone. Here, in this one body were the bodies, the brains, the power, the spirit, of those other ninety-eight men. In the fourth dimension, all the millions of third-dimensional things were one. Perhaps that particular portion of the third dimension called the Earth had sprung from, or degenerated from, one single unit of a dissolving, worn-out fourth dimension. The third dimension, warped back to a higher plane, was automatically obeying the mystic laws of evolution by reforming in the shape of that old ancestor, unimaginably removed in time from the race he had begot. He was no longer Henry Woods, newspaperman; he was an entity that had given birth, in the dim ages when the Earth was born, to a third dimension. Nor was he alone. This body of his was composed of other sons of that ancient entity.

He felt himself grow, felt his body grow vaster, assume greater proportions, felt new vitality flow through him. It was the other men, the men who were flinging themselves into the column of light in the laboratory to be warped back to this plane, to be incorporated in his body.

It was not his body, however. His brain was not his alone. The pronoun, he realized, represented the sum total of those other men, his fellow adventurers.

Suddenly a new feeling came, a feeling of completeness, a feeling of supreme fitness. He knew that the last of the ninety-eight men had stepped across the disk, that all were here in this giant body.

Now he could see more clearly. Things in the landscape, which had escaped him before, became recognizable. Awful thoughts ran through his brain, heavy, ponderous, black thoughts. He began to recognize the landscape as something familiar, something he had seen before, a thing with which he was intimate. Phenomena, which his third-dimensional intelligence would have gasped at, became commonplace. He was finally seeing through fourth-dimensional eyes, thinking fourth-dimensional thoughts.

Memory seeped into his brain and he had fleeting visions, visions of dark caverns lit by hellish flames, of huge seas that battered remorselessly with mile-high waves against towering headlands that reared titanic toward a glowering sky. He remembered a red desert scattered with scarlet boulders, he remembered silver cliffs of gleaming metallic stone. Through all his thoughts ran something else, a scarlet thread of hate, an all-consuming passion, a fierce lust after the life of some other entity.

He was no longer a composite thing built of third-dimensional beings. He was a creature of another plane, a creature with a consuming hate, and suddenly he knew against whom this hate was directed and why. He knew also that this creature was near and his great fists closed and then spread wide as he knew it. How did he know it? Perhaps through some sense which he, as a being of another plane, held, but which was alien to the Earth. Later, he asked himself this question. At the time, however, there was no questioning on his part. He only knew that somewhere near was a hated enemy and he did not question the source of his knowledge. . . .

Mumbling in an idiom incomprehensible to a third-dimensional being, filled with rage that wove redly through his brain, he lumbered down the hill onto the moor, his great strides eating up the distance, his footsteps shaking the ground.

At the foot of the hill he halted and from his throat issued a challenging roar that made the very crags surrounding the moor tremble. The rocks flung back the roar as if in mockery.

Again he shouted and in the shout he framed a lurid insult to the enemy that lurked there in the cliffs.

Again the crags flung back the insult, but this time the echoes, booming over the moor, were drowned by another voice, the voice of the enemy.

At the far end of the moor appeared a gigantic form, a form that shambled on grotesque, misshapen feet, growling angrily as he came.

He came rapidly despite his clumsy gait, and as he came he mouthed terrific threats.

Close to the other he halted and only then did recognition dawn in his eyes.

"*You, Mal Shaff?*" he growled in his guttural tongue, and surprise and consternation were written large upon his ugly face.

"Yes, it is I, Mal Shaff," boomed the other. "Remember, Ouglat, the day you destroyed me and my plane. I have returned to wreak my vengeance. I have solved a mystery you have never guessed and I have come back. You did not imagine you were attacking me again when you sent your minions to that other plane to feed upon the beings there. It was I you were attacking, fool, and I am here to kill you."

Ouglat leaped and the thing that had been Henry Woods, newspaperman, and ninety-eight other men, but was now Mal Shaff of the fourth dimension, leaped to meet him.

Mal Shaff felt the force of Ouglat, felt the sharp pain of a hammering fist, and lashed out with those horrible arms of his to smash at the leering face of his antagonist. He felt his fists strike solid flesh, felt the bones creak and tremble beneath his blow.

His nostrils were filled with the terrible stench of the other's foul breath and his filthy body. He teetered on his gnarled legs and side-stepped a vicious kick and then stepped in to gouge with straightened thumb at the other's eye. The thumb went true and Ouglat howled in pain.

Mal Shaff leaped back as his opponent charged head down, and his knotted fist beat a thunderous tattoo as the misshapen beast closed in. He felt clawing fingers seeking his throat, felt ghastly nails ripping at his shoulders. In desperation he struck blindly, and Ouglat reeled away. With a quick stride he shortened the distance between them and struck Ouglat a hard blow squarely on his slavering mouth. Pressing hard upon the reeling figure, he swung his fists like sledge-hammers, and Ouglat stumbled, falling in a heap on the sand.

Mal Shaff leaped upon the fallen foe and kicked him with his taloned feet, ripping him wickedly. There was no thought of fair play, no faintest glimmer of mercy. This was a battle to the death: there could be no quarter.

The fallen monster howled, but his voice cut short as his foul mouth, with its razor-edged fangs, closed on the other's body. His talons, seeking a hold, clawed deep.

Mal Shaff, his brain a screaming maelstrom of weird emotions, aimed pile-driver blows at the enemy, clawed and ripped. Together the two rolled, locked tight in titanic battle, on the sandy plain and a great cloud of heavy dust marked where they struggled.

In desperation Ouglat put every ounce of his strength into a heave that broke the other's grip and flung him away.

The two monstrosities surged to their feet, their eyes red with hate, glaring through the dust cloud at one another.

Slowly Ouglat's hand stole to a black, wicked cylinder that hung on a belt at his waist. His fingers closed upon it and he drew the weapon. As he leveled it at Mal Shaff, his lips curled back and his features distorted into something that was not pleasant to see.

Mal Shaff, with doubled fists, saw the great thumb of his enemy slowly depressing a button on the cylinder, and a great fear held him rooted in his tracks. In the back of his brain something was vainly trying to explain to him the horror of this thing which the other held.

Then a multicolored spiral, like a corkscrew column of vapor, sprang from the cylinder and flashed toward him. It struck him full on the chest and even as it did so he caught the ugly fire of triumph in the red eyes of his enemy.

He felt a stinging sensation where the spiral struck, but that was all. He was astounded. He had feared this weapon, had been sure it portended some form of horrible death. But all it did was to produce a slight sting.

For a split second he stood stock-still, then he surged forward and advanced upon Ouglat, his hands outspread like claws. From his throat came those horrible sounds, the speech of the fourth dimension.

"Did I not tell you, foul son of Sargouthe, that I had solved a mystery you have never guessed at? Although you destroyed me long ago, I have returned. Throw away your puny weapon. I am of the lower dimension and am invulnerable to your engines of destruction. You bloated. . . ." His words trailed off into a stream of vileness that could never have occurred to a third-dimensional mind.

Ouglat, with every line of his face distorted with fear, flung the weapon from him, and turning, fled clumsily down the moor, with Mal Shaff at his heels.

Steadily Mal Shaff gained and with only a few feet separating him from Ouglat, he dived with outspread arms at the other's legs.

The two came down together, but Mal Shaff's grip was broken by the fall and the two regained their feet at almost the same instant.

The wild moor resounded to their throaty roaring and the high cliffs flung back the echoes of the bellowing of the two gladiators below. It was sheer strength now and flesh and bone were bruised and broken under the life-shaking blows that they dealt. Great furrows were plowed in the sand by the sliding of heavy feet as the two fighters shifted to or away from attack. Blood, blood of fourth-dimensional creatures, covered the bodies of the two and stained the sand with its horrible hue. Perspiration streamed from them and their breath came in gulping gasps.

The lurid sun slid across the purple sky and still the two fought on. Ouglat, one of the ancients, and Mal Shaff, reincarnated. It was a battle of giants, a battle that must have beggared even the titanic tilting of forgotten gods and entities in the ages when the third-dimensional Earth was young.

Mal Shaff had no conception of time. He may have fought seconds or hours. It seemed an eternity. He had attempted to fight scientifically, but had failed to do so. While one part of him had cried out to elude his opponent, to wait for openings, to conserve his strength, another part had shouted at him to step in and smash, smash, smash at the hated monstrosity pitted against him.

It seemed Ouglat was growing in size, had become more agile, that his strength was greater. His punches hurt more; it was harder to hit him.

Still Mal Shaff drilled in determinedly, head down, fists working like pistons. As the other seemed to grow stronger and larger, he seemed to become smaller and weaker.

It was queer. Ouglat should be tired, too. His punches should be weaker. He should move more slowly, be heavier on his feet.

There was no doubt of it. Ouglat was growing larger, was drawing on some mysterious reserve of strength. From somewhere new force and life were flowing into his body. But from where was this strength coming?

A huge fist smashed against Mal Shaff's jaw. He felt himself lifted, and the next moment he skidded across the sand.

Lying there, gasping for breath, almost too fagged to rise, with the black bulk of the enemy looming through the dust cloud before him, he suddenly realized the source of the other's renewed strength.

Ouglat was recalling his minions from the third dimension! They were incorporating in his body, returning to their parent body!

They were coming back from the third dimension to the fourth dimension to fight a third-dimensional thing reincarnated in the fourth-dimensional form it had lost millions of eons ago!

This was the end, thought Mal Shaff. But he staggered to his feet to meet the charge of the ancient enemy and a grim song, a death chant immeasurably old, suddenly and dimly remembered from out of the mists of countless millenniums, was on his lips as he swung a pile-driver blow into the suddenly astonished face of the rushing Ouglat. . . .

The milky globe atop the machine in Dr. White's laboratory glowed softly, and within that glow two figures seemed to struggle.

Before the machine, his hands still on the controls, stood Dr. Silas White. Behind him the room was crowded with newspapermen and photographers.

Hours had passed since the ninety-eight men—ninety-nine, counting Henry Woods—had stepped into the brittle column of light to be shunted back through unguessed time to a different plane of existence. The old scientist, during all those hours, had stood like a graven image before his machine, eyes staring fixedly at the globe.

Through the open windows he had heard the cry of the newsboy as the *Press* put the greatest scoop of all time on the street. The phone had rung like mad and George answered it. The doorbell buzzed repeatedly and George ushered in newspapermen who had asked innumerable questions, to which he had replied briefly, almost mechanically. The reporters had fought for the use of the one phone in the house and had finally drawn lots for it. A few had raced out to use other phones.

Photographers came and flashes popped and cameras clicked. The room was in an uproar. On the rare occasions when the reporters were not using the phone the instrument buzzed shrilly. Authoritative voices demanded Dr. Silas White. George, his eyes on the old man, stated that Dr. Silas White could not be disturbed, that he was busy.

From the street below came the heavy-throated hum of thousands of voices. The street was packed with a jostling crowd of awed humanity, every eye fastened on the house of Dr. Silas White. Lines of police held them back.

"What makes them move so slowly?" asked a reporter, staring at the globe. "They hardly seem to be moving. It looks like a slow motion picture."

"They are not moving slowly," replied Dr. White. "There must be a difference in time in the fourth dimension. Maybe what is hours to us is only seconds to them. Time must flow more slowly there. Perhaps it is a bigger place than this third plane. That may account for it. They aren't moving slowly, they are fighting savagely. It's a fight to the death! Watch!"

The grotesque arm of one of the figures in the milky globe was moving out slowly, loafing along, aimed at the head of the other. Slowly the other twisted his body aside, but too slowly. The fist finally touched the head, still moving slowly forward, the body following as slowly. The head of the creature twisted, bent backward, and the body toppled back in a leisurely manner.

"What does White say? . . . Can't you get a statement of some sort from him? Won't he talk at all? A hell of a fine reporter you are—can't even get a man to open his mouth. Ask him about Henry Woods. Get a human-interest slant on Woods walking into the light. Ask him how long this is going to last. Damn it all, man, do something, and don't bother me again until you have a real story—yes, I said a real story—are you hard of hearing? For God's sake, do something!"

The editor slammed the receiver on the hook.

"Brooks," he snapped, "get the War Department at Washington. Ask them if they're going to back up White. Go on, go on. Get busy. . . . How will you get them? I don't know. Just get them, that's all. Get them!"

Typewriters gibbered like chuckling morons through the roaring tumult of the editorial rooms. Copy boys rushed about, white sheets clutched in their grimy hands. Telephones jangled and strident voices blared through the haze that arose from the pipes and cigarettes of perspiring writers who feverishly transferred to paper the startling events that were rocking the world.

The editor, his necktie off, his shirt open, his sleeves rolled to the elbow, drummed his fingers on the desk. It had been a hectic twenty-four hours and he had stayed at the desk every minute of the time. He was dead tired. When the moment of relaxation came, when the tension snapped, he knew he would fall into an exhausted stupor of sleep, but the excitement was keeping him on his feet. There was work to do. There was news such as the world had never known before. Each new story meant a new front make-up, another extra. Even now the presses were thundering, even now papers with the ink hardly dry upon them were being snatched by the avid public from the hands of screaming newsboys.

A man raced toward the city desk, waving a sheet of paper in his hand. Sensing something unusual the others in the room crowded about as he laid the sheet before the editor.

"Just came in," the man gasped.

The paper was a wire dispatch. It read:

"Rome—The Black Horror is in full retreat. Although still apparently immune to the weapons being used against it, it is lifting the siege of this city. The cause is unknown."

The editor ran his eye down the sheet. There was another dateline:

"Madrid—The Black Horror, which has enclosed this city in a ring of dark terror for the last two days, is fleeing, rapidly disappearing. . . ."

The editor pressed a button. There was an answering buzz.

"Composing room," he shouted, "get ready for a new front! Yes, another extra. This will knock their eyes out!"

A telephone jangled furiously. The editor seized it.

"Yes. What was that? . . . White says he must have help. I see. Woods and the others are weakening. Being badly beaten, eh? . . . More men needed to go out to the other plane. Wants reinforcements. Yes. I see. Well, tell him that he'll have them. If he can wait half an hour we'll have them walking by thousands into that light. I'll be damned if we won't! Just tell White to hang on! We'll have the whole nation coming to the rescue!"

He jabbed up the receiver.

"Richards," he said, "write a streamer, 'Help Needed,' 'Reinforcements Called'—something of that sort, you know. Make it scream. Tell the foreman to dig out the biggest type he has. A foot high. If we ever needed big type, we need it now!"

He turned to the telephone.

"Operator," he said, "get me the Secretary of War at Washington. The secretary in person, you understand. No one else will do."

He turned again to the reporters who stood about the desk.

"In two hours," he explained, banging the desk top for emphasis, "we'll have the United States Army marching into that light Woods walked into!"

The bloody sun was touching the edge of the weird world, seeming to hesitate before taking the final plunge behind the towering black crags that hung above the ink-pot shadows at their base. The purple sky had darkened until it was almost the color of soft, black velvet. Great stars were blazing out.

Ouglat loomed large in the gathering twilight, a horrible misshapen ogre of an outer world. He had grown taller, broader, greater. Mal Shaff's head now was on a level with the other's chest; his huge arms seemed toylike in comparison with those of Ouglat, his legs mere pipestems.

Time and time again he had barely escaped as the clutching hands of Ouglat reached out to grasp him. Once within those hands he would be torn apart.

The battle had become a game of hide and seek, a game of cat and mouse, with Mal Shaff the mouse.

Slowly the sun sank and the world became darker. His brain working feverishly, Mal Shaff waited for the darkness. Adroitly he worked the battle nearer and nearer to the Stygian darkness that lay at the foot of the mighty crags. In the darkness he might escape. He could no longer continue this unequal fight. Only escape was left.

The sun was gone now. Blackness was dropping swiftly over the land, like a great blanket, creating the illusion of the glowering sky descending to the ground. Only a few feet away lay the total blackness under the cliffs.

Like a flash Mal Shaff darted into the blackness, was completely swallowed in it. Roaring, Ouglat followed.

His shoulders almost touching the great rock wall that shot straight up hundreds of feet above him, Mal Shaff ran swiftly, fear lending speed to his shivering legs. Behind him he heard the bellowing of his enemy. Ouglat was searching for him, a hopeless search in that total darkness. He would never find him. Mal Shaff felt sure.

Fagged and out of breath, he dropped panting at the foot of the wall. Blood pounded through his head and his strength seemed to be gone. He lay still and stared out into the less dark moor that stretched before him.

For some time he lay there, resting. Aimlessly he looked out over the moor, and then he suddenly noted, some distance to his right, a hill rising from the moor. The hill was vaguely familiar. He remembered it dimly as being of great importance.

A sudden inexplicable restlessness filled him. Far behind him he heard the enraged bellowing of Ouglat, but that he scarcely noticed. So long as darkness lay upon the land he knew he was safe from his enemy.

The hill had made him restless. He must reach the top. He could think of no logical reason for doing so. Obviously he was safer here at the base of the cliff, but a voice seemed to be calling, a friendly voice from the hilltop.

He rose on aching legs and forged ahead. Every fiber of his being cried out in protest, but resolutely he placed one foot ahead of the other, walking mechanically.

Opposite the hill he disregarded the strange call that pulsed down upon him, long enough to rest his tortured body. He must build up his strength for the climb.

He realized that danger lay ahead. Once he quitted the blackness of the cliff's base, Ouglat, even in the darkness that lay over the land, might see him. That would be disastrous. Once over the top of the hill he would be safe.

Suddenly the landscape was bathed in light, a soft green radiance. One moment it had been pitch dark, the next it was light, as if a giant search-light had been snapped on.

In terror, Mal Shaff looked for the source of the light. Just above the horizon hung a great green orb, which moved up the ladder of the sky even as he watched.

A moon! A huge green satellite hurtling swiftly around this cursed world!

A great, overwhelming fear sat upon Mal Shaff and with a high, shrill scream of anger he raced forward, forgetful of aching body and outraged lungs.

His scream was answered from far off, and out of the shadows of the cliffs toward the far end of the moor a black figure hurled itself. Ouglat was on the trail!

Mal Shaff tore madly up the slope, topped the crest, and threw himself flat on the ground, almost exhausted.

A queer feeling stole over him, a queer feeling of well-being. New strength was flowing into him, the old thrill of battle was pounding through his blood once more.

Not only were queer things happening to his body, but also to his brain. The world about him looked queer, held a sort of an intangible mystery he could not understand. A half question formed in the back of his brain. Who and what was he? Queer thoughts to be thinking! He was Mal Shaff, but had he always been Mal Shaff?

He remembered a brittle column of light, creatures with bodies unlike his body, walking into it. He had been one of those creatures. There was something about dimensions, about different planes, a plan for one plane to attack another!

He scrambled to his bowed legs and beat his great chest with mighty, long-nailed hands. He flung back his head and from his throat broke a sound to curdle the blood of even the bravest.

On the moor below Ouglat heard the cry and answered it with one equally ferocious.

Mal Shaff took a step forward, then stopped stock-still. Through his brain went a sharp command to return to the spot where he had stood, to wait there until attacked. He stepped back, shifting his feet impatiently.

He was growing larger; every second fresh vitality was pouring into him. Before his eyes danced a red curtain of hate and his tongue roared forth a series of insulting challenges to the figure that was even now approaching the foot of the hill.

As Ouglat climbed the hill, the night became an insane bedlam. The challenging roars beat like surf against the black cliffs.

Ouglat's lips were flecked with foam, his red eyes were mere slits, his mouth worked convulsively.

They were only a few feet apart when Ouglat charged.

Mal Shaff was ready for him. There was no longer any difference in their size and they met like the two forward walls of contending football teams.

Mal Shaff felt the soft throat of the other under his fingers and his grip tightened. Maddened, Ouglat shot terrific blow after terrific blow into Mal Shaff's body.

Try as he might, however, he could not shake the other's grip.

It was silent now. The night seemed brooding, watching the struggle on the hilltop.

Larger and larger grew Mal Shaff, until he overtopped Ouglat like a giant.

Then he loosened his grip and, as Ouglat tried to scuttle away, reached down to grasp him by the nape of his neck.

High above his head he lifted his enemy and dashed him to the ground. With a leap he was on the prostrate figure, trampling it apart, smashing it into the ground. With wild cries he stamped the earth, treading out the last of Ouglat, the Black Horror.

When no trace of the thing that had been Ouglat remained, he moved away and viewed the trampled ground.

Then, for the first time he noticed that the crest of the hill was crowded with other monstrous figures. He glared at them, half in surprise, half in anger. He had not noticed their silent approach.

"It is Mal Shaff!" cried one.

"Yes, I am Mal Shaff. What do you want?"

"But, Mal Shaff, Ouglat destroyed you once long ago!"

"And I, just now," replied Mal Shaff, "have destroyed Ouglat."

The figures were silent, shifting uneasily. Then one stepped forward.

"Mal Shaff," it said, "we thought you were dead. Apparently it was not so. We welcome you to our land again. Ouglat, who once tried to kill you and apparently failed, you have killed, which is right and proper. Come and live with us again in peace. We welcome you."

Mal Shaff bowed.

Gone was all thought of the third dimension. Through Mal Shaff's mind raced strange, haunting memories of a red desert scattered with scarlet boulders, of silver cliffs of gleaming metallic stone, of huge seas battering against towering headlands. There were other things, too. Great palaces of shining jewels, and weird nights of inhuman joy where hellish flames lit deep, black caverns.

He bowed again.

"I thank you, Bathazar," he said.

Without a backward look he shambled down the hill with the others.

"Yes?" said the editor. "What's that you say? Doctor White is dead! A suicide! Yeah, I understand. Worry, hey! Here, Roberts, take this story."

He handed over the phone.

"When you write it," he said, "play up the fact he was worried about not being able to bring the men back to the third dimension. Give him plenty of praise for ending the Black Horror. It's a big story."

"Sure," said Roberts, then spoke into the phone: "All right, Bill, shoot the works."

PROJECT MASTODON

I

The chief of protocol said, "Mr. Hudson of—ah—Mastodonia."

The secretary of state held out his hand. "I'm glad to see you, Mr. Hudson. I understand you've been here several times."

"That's right," said Hudson. "I had a hard time making your people believe I was in earnest."

"And are you, Mr. Hudson?"

"Believe me, sir, I would not try to fool you."

"And this Mastodonia," said the secretary, reaching down to tap the document upon the desk. "You will pardon me, but I've never heard of it."

"It's a new nation," Hudson explained, "but quite legitimate. We have a constitution, a democratic form of government, duly elected officials, and a code of laws. We are a free, peace-loving people and we are possessed of a vast amount of natural resources and—"

"Please tell me, sir," interrupted the secretary, "just where are you located?"

"Technically, you are our nearest neighbors."

"But that is ridiculous!" exploded Protocol.

"Not at all," insisted Hudson. "If you will give me a moment, Mr. Secretary, I have considerable evidence."

He brushed the fingers of Protocol off his sleeve and stepped forward to the desk, laying down the portfolio he carried.

"Go ahead, Mr. Hudson," said the secretary. "Why don't we all sit down and be comfortable while we talk this over?"

"You have my credentials, I see. Now here is a propos—"

"I have a document signed by a certain Wesley Adams."

"He's our first president," said Hudson. "Our George Washington, you might say."

"What is the purpose of this visit, Mr. Hudson?"

"We'd like to establish diplomatic relations. We think it would be to our mutual benefit. After all, we are a sister republic in perfect sympathy with your policies and aims. We'd like to negotiate trade agreements and we'd be grateful for some Point Four aid."

The secretary smiled. "Naturally. Who doesn't?"

"We're prepared to offer something in return," Hudson told him stiffly. "For one thing, we could offer sanctuary."

"Sanctuary!"

"I understand," said Hudson, "that in the present state of international tensions, a foolproof sanctuary is not something to be sneezed at."

The secretary turned stone cold. "I'm an extremely busy man."

Protocol took Hudson firmly by the arm. "Out you go."

General Leslie Bowers put in a call to State and got the secretary.

"I don't like to bother you, Herb," he said, "but there's something I want to check. Maybe you can help me."

"Glad to help you if I can."

"There's a fellow hanging around out here at the Pentagon, trying to get in to see me. Said I was the only one he'd talk to, but you know how it is."

"I certainly do."

"Name of Huston or Hudson or something like that."

"He was here just an hour or so ago," said the secretary. "Crackpot sort of fellow."

"He's gone now?"

"Yes. I don't think he'll be back."

"Did he say where you could reach him?"

"No, I don't believe he did."

"How did he strike you? I mean what kind of impression did you get of him?"

"I told you. A crackpot."

"I suppose he is. He said something to one of the colonels that got me worrying. Can't pass up anything, you know—not in the Dirty Tricks Department. Even if it's crackpot, these days you got to have a look at it."

"He offered sanctuary," said the secretary indignantly. "Can you imagine that!"

"He's been making the rounds, I guess," the general said. "He was over at AEC. Told them some sort of tale about knowing where there were vast uranium deposits. It was the AEC that told me he was heading your way."

"We get them all the time. Usually we can ease them out. This Hudson was just a little better than the most of them. He got in to see me."

"He told the colonel something about having a plan that would enable us to establish secret bases anywhere we wished, even in the territory of potential enemies. I know it sounds crazy. . . ."

"Forget it, Les."

"You're probably right," said the general, "but this idea sends me. Can you imagine the look on their Iron Curtain faces?"

The scared little government clerk, darting conspiratorial glances all about him, brought the portfolio to the FBI.

"I found it in a bar down the street," he told the man who took him in tow. "Been going there for years. And I found this portfolio laying in the booth. I saw the man who must have left it there and I tried to find him later, but I couldn't."

"How do you know he left it there?"

"I just figured he did. He left the booth just as I came in and it was sort of dark in there and it took a minute to see this thing laying there. You see, I always take the same booth every day and Joe sees me come in and he brings me the usual and—"

"You saw this man leave the booth you usually sit in?"

"That's right."

"Then you saw the portfolio."

"Yes, sir."

"You tried to find the man, thinking it must have been his."

"That's exactly what I did."

"But by the time you went to look for him, he had disappeared."

"That's the way it was."

"Now tell me—why did you bring it here? Why didn't you turn it in to the management so the man could come back and claim it?"

"Well, sir, it was like this. I had a drink or two and I was wondering all the time what was in that portfolio. So finally I took a peek and—"

"And what you saw decided you to bring it here to us."

"That's right. I saw—"

"Don't tell me what you saw. Give me your name and address and don't say anything about this. You understand that we're grateful to you for thinking of us, but we'd rather you said nothing."

"Mum's the word," the little clerk assured him, full of vast importance.

The FBI phoned Dr. Ambrose Amberly, Smithsonian expert on paleontology.

"We've got something, Doctor, that we'd like you to have a look at. A lot of movie film."

"I'll be most happy to. I'll come down as soon as I get clear. End of the week, perhaps?"

"This is very urgent, Doctor. Damnest thing you ever saw. Big, shaggy elephants and tigers with teeth down to their necks. There's a beaver the size of a bear."

"Fakes," said Amberly, disgusted. "Clever gadgets. Camera angles."

"That's what we thought first, but there are no gadgets, no camera angles. This is the real McCoy."

"I'm on my way," the paleontologist said, hanging up.

Snide item in smug, smartaleck gossip column: Saucers are passé at the Pentagon. There's another mystery that's got the high brass very high.

II

President Wesley Adams and Secretary of State John Cooper sat glumly under a tree in the capital of Mastodonia and waited for the ambassador extraordinary to return.

"I tell you, Wes," said Cooper, who, under various pseudonyms, was also the secretaries of commerce, treasury and war, "this is a crazy thing we did. What if Chuck can't get back? They might throw him in jail or something might happen to the time unit or the helicopter. We should have gone along."

"We had to stay," Adams said. "You know what would happen to this camp and our supplies if we weren't around here to guard them."

"The only thing that's given us any trouble is that old mastodon. If he comes around again, I'm going to take a skillet and bang him in the brisket."

"That isn't the only reason, either," said President Adams, "and you know it. We can't go deserting this nation now that we've created it. We have to keep possession. Just planting a flag and saying it's ours wouldn't be enough. We might be called upon for proof that we've established residence. Something like the old homestead laws, you know."

"We'll establish residence sure enough," growled Secretary Cooper, "if something happens to that time unit or the helicopter."

"You think they'll do it, Johnny?"

"Who do what?"

"The United States. Do you think they'll recognize us?"

"Not if they know who we are."

"That's what I'm afraid of."

"Chuck will talk them into it. He can talk the skin right off a cat."

"Sometimes I think we're going at this wrong. Sure, Chuck's got the long-range view and I suppose it's best. But maybe what we ought to do is grab a good, fast profit and get out of here. We could take in hunting parties at ten thousand a head or maybe we could lease it to a movie company."

"We can do all that and do it legally and with full protection," Cooper told him, "if we can get ourselves recognized as a sovereign nation. If we negotiate a mutual defense pact, no one would dare get hostile because we could squawk to Uncle Sam."

"All you say is true," Adams agreed, "but there are going to be questions. It isn't just a matter of walking into Washington and getting recognition. They'll want to know about us, such as our population. What if Chuck has to tell them it's a total of three persons?"

Cooper shook his head. "He wouldn't answer that way, Wes. He'd duck the question or give them some diplomatic double-talk. After all, how can we be *sure* there are only three of us? We took over the whole continent, remember."

"You know well enough, Johnny, there are no other humans back here in North America. The farthest back any scientist will place the migrations from Asia is 30,000 years. They haven't got here yet."

"Maybe we should have done it differently," mused Cooper. "Maybe we should have included the whole world in our proclamation, not just the continent. That way, we could claim quite a population."

"It wouldn't have held water. Even as it is, we went a little further than precedent allows. The old explorers usually laid claim to certain watersheds. They'd find a river and lay claim to all the territory drained by the river. They didn't go grabbing off whole continents."

"That's because they were never sure of exactly what they had," said Cooper. "We are. We have what you might call the advantage of hindsight."

He leaned back against the tree and stared across the land. It was a pretty place, he thought—the rolling ridges covered by vast grazing areas and small groves, the forest-covered, ten-mile river valley. And everywhere one looked, the grazing herds of mastodon, giant bison and wild horses, with the less gregarious fauna scattered hit and miss.

Old Buster, the troublesome mastodon, a lone bull which had been probably run out of a herd by a younger rival, stood at the edge of a grove a quarter-mile away. He had his head down and was curling and uncurling his trunk in an aimless sort of way while he teetered slowly in a lazy-crazy fashion by lifting first one foot and then another.

The old cuss was lonely, Cooper told himself. That was why he hung around like a homeless dog—except that he was too big and awkward to have much pet-appeal and, more than likely, his temper was unstable.

The afternoon sun was pleasantly warm and the air, it seemed to Cooper, was the freshest he had ever smelled. It was, altogether, a very pleasant place, an Indian-summer sort of land, ideal for a Sunday picnic or a camping trip.

The breeze was just enough to float out from its flagstaff before the tent the national banner of Mastodonia—a red rampant mastodon upon a field of green.

"You know, Johnny," said Adams, "there's one thing that worries me a lot. If we're going to base our claim on precedent, we may be way off base. The old explorers always claimed their discoveries for their nations or their king, never for themselves."

"The principle was entirely different," Cooper told him. "Nobody ever did anything for himself in those days. Everyone was always under someone else's protection. The explorers either were financed by their governments or were sponsored by them or operated under a royal charter or a patent. With us, it's different. Ours is a private enterprise. You dreamed up the time unit and built it. The three of us chipped in to buy the helicopter. We've paid all of our expenses out of our own pockets. We never got a dime from anyone. What we found is ours."

"I hope you're right," said Adams uneasily.

Old Buster had moved out from the grove and was shuffling warily toward the camp. Adams picked up the rifle that lay across his knees.

"Wait," said Cooper sharply. "Maybe he's just bluffing. It would be a shame to plaster him; he's such a nice old guy."

Adams half raised the rifle.

"I'll give him three steps more," he announced. "I've had enough of him."

Suddenly a roar burst out of the air just above their heads. The two leaped to their feet.

"It's Chuck!" Cooper yelled. "He's back!"

The helicopter made a half-turn of the camp and came rapidly to Earth.

Trumpeting with terror, Old Buster was a dwindling dot far down the grassy ridge.

III

They built the nightly fires circling the camp to keep out the animals.

"It'll be the death of me yet," said Adams wearily, "cutting all this wood."

"We have to get to work on that stockade," Cooper said. "We've fooled around too long. Some night, fire or no fire, a herd of mastodon will come busting in here and if they ever hit the helicopter, we'll be dead ducks. It wouldn't take more than just five seconds to turn us into Robinson Crusoes of the Pleistocene."

"Well, now that this recognition thing has petered out on us," said Adams, "maybe we can get down to business."

"Trouble is," Cooper answered, "we spent about the last of our money on the chain saw to cut this wood and on Chuck's trip to Washington. To build a stockade, we need a tractor. We'd kill ourselves if we tried to rassle that many logs bare-handed."

"Maybe we could catch some of those horses running around out there."

"Have you ever broken a horse?"

"No, that's one thing I never tried."

"Me, either. How about you, Chuck?"

"Not me," said the ex-ambassador extraordinary bluntly.

Cooper squatted down beside the coals of the cooking fire and twirled the spit. Upon the spit were three grouse and half a dozen quail. The huge coffee pot was sending out a nose-tingling aroma. Biscuits were baking in the reflector.

"We've been here six weeks," he said, "and we're still living in a tent and cooking on an open fire. We better get busy and get something done."

"The stockade first," said Adams, "and that means a tractor."

"We could use the helicopter."

"Do you want to take the chance? That's our getaway. Once something happens to it. . . ."

"I guess not," Cooper admitted, gulping.

"We could use some of that Point Four aid right now," commented Adams.

"They threw me out," said Hudson. "Everywhere I went, sooner or later they got around to throwing me out. They were real organized about it."

"Well, we tried," Adams said.

"And to top it off," added Hudson, "I had to go and lose all that film and now we'll have to waste our time taking more of it. Personally, I don't ever want to let another saber-tooth get that close to me while I hold the camera."

"You didn't have a thing to worry about," Adams objected. "Johnny was right there behind you with the gun."

"Yeah, with the muzzle about a foot from my head when he let go."

"I stopped him, didn't I?" demanded Cooper.

"With his head right in my lap."

"Maybe we won't have to take any more pictures," Adams suggested.

"We'll have to," Cooper said. "There are sportsmen up ahead who'd fork over ten thousand bucks easy for two weeks of hunting here. But before we could sell them on it, we'd have to show them movies. That scene with the saber-tooth would cinch it."

"If it didn't scare them off," Hudson pointed out. "The last few feet showed nothing but the inside of his throat."

Ex-ambassador Hudson looked unhappy. "I don't like the whole setup. As soon as we bring someone in, the news is sure to leak. And once the word gets out, there'll be guys lying in ambush for us—maybe even nations—scheming to steal the know-how, legally or violently. That's what scares me the most about those films I lost. Someone will find them and they may guess what it's all about, but I'm hoping they either won't believe it or can't manage to trace us."

"We could swear the hunting parties to secrecy," said Cooper.

"How could a sportsman keep still about the mounted head of a saber-tooth or a record piece of ivory?" And the same thing would apply to anyone we approached. Some university could raise dough to send a team of scientists back here and a movie company would cough up plenty to use this place as a location for a caveman epic. But it wouldn't be worth a thing to either of them if they couldn't tell about it.

"Now if we could have gotten recognition as a nation, we'd have been all set. We could make our own laws and regulations and be able to enforce them. We could bring in settlers and establish trade. We could exploit our natural resources. It would all be legal and aboveboard. We could tell who we were and where we were and what we had to offer."

"We aren't licked yet," said Adams. "There's a lot that we can do. Those river hills are covered with ginseng. We can each dig a dozen pounds a day. There's good money in the root."

"Ginseng root," Cooper said, "is peanuts. We need *big* money."

"Or we could trap," offered Adams. "The place is alive with beaver."

"Have you taken a good look at those beaver? They're about the size of a St. Bernard."

"All the better. Think how much just one pelt would bring."

"No dealer would believe that it was beaver. He'd think you were trying to pull a fast one on him. And there are only a few states that allow beaver to be trapped. To sell the pelts—even if you could—you'd have to take out licenses in each of those states."

"Those mastodon carry a lot of ivory," said Cooper. "And if we wanted to go north, we'd find mammoths that would carry even more. . . ."

"And get socked into the jug for ivory smuggling?"

They sat, all three of them, staring at the fire, not finding anything to say.

The moaning complaint of a giant hunting cat came from somewhere up the river.

IV

Hudson lay in his sleeping bag, staring at the sky. It bothered him a lot. There was not one familiar constellation, not one star that he could name with any certainty. This juggling of the stars, he thought, emphasized more than anything else in this ancient land the vast gulf of years which lay between him and the Earth where he had been—or would be—born.

A hundred and fifty thousand years, Adams had said, give or take ten thousand. There just was no way to know. Later on, there might be. A measurement of the stars and a comparison with their positions in the twentieth century might be one way of doing it. But at the moment, any figure could be no more than a guess.

The time machine was not something that could be tested for calibration or performance. As a matter of fact, there was no way to test it. They had not been certain, he remembered, the first time they had used it, that it would really work. There had been no way to find out. When it worked, you knew it worked. And if it hadn't worked, there would have been no way of knowing beforehand that it wouldn't.

Adams had been sure, of course, but that had been because he had absolute reliance in the half-mathematical, half-philosophic concepts he had worked out—concepts that neither Hudson nor Cooper could come close to understanding.

That had always been the way it had been, even when they were kids, with Wes dreaming up the deals that he and Johnny carried out. Back in those days, too, they had used time travel in their play. Out in Johnny's back yard, they had rigged up a time machine out of a wonderful collection of salvaged junk—a wooden crate, an empty five-gallon paint pail, a battered coffee maker, a bunch of discarded copper tubing, a busted steering wheel and other odds and ends. In it, they had "traveled" back to Indian-before-the-white-man land and mammoth-land and dinosaur-land and the slaughter, he remembered, had been wonderfully appalling.

But, in reality, it had been much different. There was much more to it than gunning down the weird fauna that one found.

And they should have known there would be, for they had talked about it often.

He thought of the bull session back in university and the little, usually silent kid who sat quietly in the corner, a law-school student whose last name had been Pritchard.

And after sitting silently for some time, this Pritchard kid had spoken up: "If you guys ever do travel in time, you'll run up against more than you bargain for. I don't mean the climate or the terrain or the fauna, but the economics and the politics."

They all jeered at him, Hudson remembered, and then had gone on with their talk. And after a short while, the talk had turned to women, as it always did.

He wondered where that quiet man might be. Some day, Hudson told himself, I'll have to look him up and tell him he was right.

We did it wrong, he thought. There were so many other ways we might have done it, but we'd been so sure and greedy—greedy for the triumph and the glory—and now there was no easy way to collect.

On the verge of success, they could have sought out help, gone to some large industrial concern or an educational foundation or even to the government. Like historic explorers, they could have obtained subsidization and sponsorship. Then they would have had protection, funds to do a proper job and they need not have operated on their present shoestring—one beaten-up helicopter and one time unit. They could have had several and at least one standing by in the twentieth century as a rescue unit, should that be necessary.

But that would have meant a bargain, perhaps a very hard one, and sharing with someone who had contributed nothing but the money. And there was more than money in a thing like this—there were twenty years of dreams and a great idea and the dedication to that great idea—years of work and years of disappointment and an almost fanatical refusal to give up.

Even so, thought Hudson, they had figured well enough. There had been many chances to make blunders and they'd made relatively few. All they lacked, in the last analysis, was backing.

Take the helicopter, for example. It was the one satisfactory vehicle for time traveling. You had to get up in the air to clear whatever upheavals and subsidences there had been through geologic ages. The helicopter took you up and kept you clear and gave you a chance to pick a proper landing place. Travel without it and, granting you were lucky with land surfaces, you still might materialize in the heart of some great tree or end up in a swamp or the middle of a herd of startled, savage beasts. A plane would have done as well, but back in this world, you couldn't land a plane—or you couldn't be certain that you could. A helicopter, though, could land almost anywhere.

In the time-distance they had traveled, they almost certainly had been lucky, although one could not be entirely sure just how great a part of it was luck. Wes had felt that he had not been working as blindly as it sometimes might appear. He had calibrated the unit for jumps of 50,000 years. Finer calibration, he had said realistically, would have to wait for more developmental work.

Using the 50,000-year calibrations, they had figured it out. One jump (conceding that the calibration was correct) would have landed them at the end of the Wisconsin glacial period; two jumps, at its beginning. The third would set them down toward the end of the Sangamon Interglacial and apparently it had—give or take ten thousand years or so.

They had arrived at a time when the climate did not seem to vary greatly, either hot or cold. The flora was modern enough to give them a homelike feeling. The fauna, modern and Pleistocenic, overlapped. And the surface features were little altered from the twentieth century. The rivers ran along familiar paths, the hills and bluffs looked much the same. In this corner of the Earth, at least, 150,000 years had not changed things greatly.

Boyhood dreams, Hudson thought, were wondrous. It was not often that three men who had daydreamed in their youth could follow it out to its end. But they had and here they were.

Johnny was on watch, and it was Hudson's turn next, and he'd better get to sleep. He closed his eyes, then opened them again for another look at the unfamiliar stars. The east, he saw, was flushed with silver light. Soon the Moon would rise, which was good. A man could keep a better watch when the Moon was up.

He woke suddenly, snatched upright and into full awareness by the marrow-chilling clamor that slashed across the night. The very air seemed curdled by the savage racket and, for a moment, he sat numbed by it. Then, slowly, it seemed—his brain took the noise and separated it into two distinct but intermingled categories, the deadly screaming of a cat and the maddened trumpeting of a mastodon.

The Moon was up and the countryside was flooded by its light. Cooper, he saw, was out beyond the watchfires, standing there and watching, with his rifle ready. Adams was scrambling out of his sleeping bag, swearing softly to himself. The cooking fire had burned down to a bed of mottled coals, but the watchfires still were burning and the helicopter, parked within their circle, picked up the glint of flames.

"It's Buster," Adams told him angrily. "I'd know that bellowing of his anywhere. He's done nothing but parade up and down and bellow ever since we got here. And now he seems to have gone out and found himself a saber-tooth."

Hudson zipped down his sleeping bag, grabbed up his rifle and jumped to his feet, following Adams in a silent rush to where Cooper stood.

Cooper motioned at them. "Don't break it up. You'll never see the like of it again."

Adams brought his rifle up.

Cooper knocked the barrel down.

"You fool!" he shouted. "You want them turning on us?"

Two hundred yards away stood the mastodon and, on his back, the screeching saber-tooth. The great beast reared into the air and came down with a jolt, bucking to unseat the cat, flailing the air with his massive trunk. And as he bucked, the cat struck and struck again with his gleaming teeth, aiming for the spine.

Then the mastodon crashed head downward, as if to turn a somersault, rolled and was on his feet again, closer to them now than he had been before. The huge cat had sprung off.

For a moment, the two stood facing one another. Then the tiger charged, a flowing streak of motion in the moonlight. Buster wheeled away and the cat, leaping, hit his shoulder, clawed wildly and slid off. The mastodon whipped to the attack, tusks slashing, huge feet stamping. The cat, caught a glancing blow by one of the tusks, screamed and leaped up, to land in spread-eagle fashion upon Buster's head.

Maddened with pain and fright, blinded by the tiger's raking claws, the old mastodon ran—straight toward the camp. And as he ran, he grasped the cat in his trunk and tore him from his hold, lifted him high and threw him.

"Look out!" yelled Cooper and brought his rifle up and fired.

For an instant, Hudson saw it all as if it were a single scene, motionless, one frame snatched from a fantastic movie epic—the charging mastodon, with the tiger lifted and the sound track one great blast of bloodthirsty bedlam.

Then the scene dissolved in a blur of motion. He felt his rifle thud against his shoulder, knowing he had fired, but not hearing the explosion. And the mastodon was almost on top of him, bearing down like some mighty and remorseless engine of blind destruction.

He flung himself to one side and the giant brushed past him. Out of the tail of his eye, he saw the thrown saber-tooth crash to Earth within the circle of the watchfires.

He brought his rifle up again and caught the area behind Buster's ear within his sights. He pressed the trigger. The mastodon staggered, then regained his stride and went rushing on. He hit one of the watchfires dead center and went through it, scattering coals and burning brands.

Then there was a thud and the screeching clang of metal.

"Oh, no!" shouted Hudson.

Rushing forward, they stopped inside the circle of the fires.

The helicopter lay tilted at a crazy angle. One of its rotor blades was crumpled. Half across it, as if he might have fallen as he tried to bull his mad way over it, lay the mastodon.

Something crawled across the ground toward them, its spitting, snarling mouth gaping in the firelight, its back broken, hind legs trailing.

Calmly, without a word, Adams put a bullet into the head of the saber-tooth.

V

General Leslie Bowers rose from his chair and paced up and down the room. He stopped to bang the conference table with a knotted fist.

"You can't do it," he bawled at them. "You can't kill the project. I *know* there's something to it. We can't give it up!"

"But it's been ten years, General," said the secretary of the army. "If they were coming back, they'd be here by now."

The general stopped his pacing, stiffened. Who did that little civilian squirt think he was, talking to the military in that tone of voice!

"We know how you feel about it, General," said the chairman of the joint chiefs of staff. "I think we all recognize how deeply you're involved. You've blamed yourself all these years and there is no need of it. After all, there may be nothing to it."

"Sir," said the general, "I *know* there's something to it. I thought so at the time, even when no one else did. And what we've turned up since serves to bear me out. Let's take a look at these three men of ours. We knew almost nothing of them at the time, but we know them now. I've traced out their lives from the time that they were born until they disappeared—and I might add that, on the chance it might be all a hoax, we've searched for them for years and we've found no trace at all.

"I've talked with those who knew them and I've studied their scholastic and military records. I've arrived at the conclusion that if any three men could do it, they were the ones who could. Adams was the brains and the other two were the ones who carried out the things that he dreamed up. Cooper was a bulldog sort of man who could keep them going and it would be Hudson who would figure out the angles.

"And they knew the angles, gentlemen. They had it all doped out.

"What Hudson tried here in Washington is substantial proof of that. But even back in school, they were thinking of those angles. I talked some years ago to a lawyer in New York, name of Pritchard. He told me that even back in university, they talked of the economic and political problems that they might face if they ever cracked what they were working at.

"Wesley Adams was one of our brightest young scientific men. His record at the university and his war work bears that out. After the war, there were at least a dozen jobs he could have had. But he wasn't interested. And I'll tell you why he wasn't. He had something bigger—something he wanted to work on. So he and these two others went off by themselves—"

"You think he was working on a temporal—" the army secretary cut in.

"He was working on a time machine," roared the general. "I don't know about this 'temporal' business. Just plain 'time machine' is good enough for me."

"Let's calm down, General," said the JCS chairman, "After all, there's no need to shout."

The general nodded. "I'm sorry, sir. I get all worked up about this. I've spent the last ten years with it. As you say, I'm trying to make up for what I failed to do ten years ago. I should have talked to Hudson. I was busy, sure, but not that busy. It's an official state of mind that we're too busy to see anyone and I plead guilty on that score. And now that you're talking about closing the project—"

"It's costing us money," said the army secretary.

"And we have no direct evidence," pointed out the JCS chairman.

"I don't know what you want," snapped the general. "If there was any man alive who could crack time, that man was Wesley Adams. We found where he worked. We found the workshop and we talked to neighbors who said there was something funny going on and—"

"But ten years, General!" the army secretary protested.

"Hudson came here, bringing us the greatest discovery in all history, and we kicked him out. After that, do you expect them to come crawling back to us?"

"You think they went to someone else?"

"They wouldn't do that. They know what the thing they have found would mean. They wouldn't sell us out."

"Hudson came with a preposterous proposition," said the man from the state department.

"They had to protect themselves!" yelled the general. "If you had discovered a virgin planet with its natural resources intact, what would you do about it? Come trotting down here and hand it over to a government that's too 'busy' to recognize—"

"General!"

"Yes, sir," apologized the general tiredly. "I wish you gentlemen could see my view of it, how it all fits together. First there were the films and we have the word of a dozen competent paleontologists that it's impossible to fake anything as perfect as those films. But even granting that they could be, there are certain differences that no one would ever think of faking, because no one ever knew. Who, as an example, would put lynx tassels on the ears of a saber-tooth? Who would know that young mastodon were black?

"And the location. I wonder if you've forgotten that we tracked down the location of Adams' workshop from those films alone. They gave us clues so positive that we didn't even hesitate— we drove straight to the old deserted farm where Adams and his friends had worked. Don't you see how it all fits together?"

"I presume," the man from the state department said nastily, "that you even have an explanation as to why they chose that particular location."

"You thought you had me there," said the general, "but I have an answer. A good one. The southwestern corner of Wisconsin is a geologic curiosity. It was missed by all the glaciations. Why, we do not know. Whatever the reason, the glaciers came down on both sides of it and far to the south of it and left it standing there, a little island in a sea of ice.

"And another thing: Except for a time in the Triassic, that same area of Wisconsin has always been dry land. That and a few other spots are the only areas in North America which have not, time and time again, been covered by water. I don't think it necessary to point out the comfort it would be to an experimental traveler in time to be certain that, in almost any era he might hit, he'd have dry land beneath him."

The economics expert spoke up: "We've given this matter a lot of study and, while we do not feel ourselves competent to rule upon the possibility or impossibility of time travel, there are some observations I should like, at some time, to make."

"Go ahead right now," said the JCS chairman.

"We see one objection to the entire matter. One of the reasons, naturally, that we had some interest in it is that, if true, it would give us an entire new planet to exploit, perhaps more wisely than we've done in the past. But the thought occurs that any planet has only a certain grand total of natural resources. If we go into the past and exploit them, what effect will that have upon what is left of those resources for use in the present? Wouldn't we, in doing this, be robbing ourselves of our own heritage?"

"That contention," said the AEC chairman, "wouldn't hold true in every case. Quite the reverse, in fact. We know that there was, in some geologic ages in the past, a great deal more uranium than we have today. Go back far enough and you'd catch that uranium before it turned into lead. In southwestern Wisconsin, there is a lot of lead. Hudson told us he knew the location of vast uranium deposits and we thought he was a crackpot talking through his hat. If we'd known—let's be fair about this—if we had known and believed him about going back in time, we'd have snapped him up at once and all this would not have happened."

"It wouldn't hold true with forests, either," said the chairman of the JCS. "Or with pastures or with crops."

The economics expert was slightly flushed. "There is another thing," he said. "If we go back in time and colonize the land we find there, what would happen when that—well, let's call it retroactive—when that retroactive civilization reaches the beginning of our historic period? What will result from that cultural collision? Will our history change? Is what has happened false? Is all—"

"That's all poppycock!" the general shouted. "That and this other talk about using up resources. Whatever we did in the past— or are about to do—has been done already. I've lain awake nights, mister, thinking about all these things and there is no answer, believe me, except the one I give you. The question which faces us here is an immediate one. Do we give all this up or do we keep on watching that Wisconsin farm, waiting for them to come back? Do we keep on trying to find, independently, the process or formula or method that Adams found for traveling in time?"

"We've had no luck in our research so far, General," said the quiet physicist who sat at the table's end. "If you were not so sure and if the evidence were not so convincing that it had been done by Adams, I'd say flatly that it is impossible. We have no approach which holds any hope at all. What we've done so far, you might best describe as flounder. But if Adams turned the trick, it must be possible. There may be, as a matter of fact, more ways than one. We'd like to keep on trying."

"Not one word of blame has been put on you for your failure," the chairman told the physicist. "That you could do it seems to be more than can be humanly expected. If Adams did it—*if* he did, I say—it must have been simply that he blundered on an avenue of research no other man has thought of."

"You will recall," said the general, "that the research program, even from the first, was thought of strictly as a gamble. Our one hope was, and must remain, that they will return."

"It would have been so much simpler all around," the state department man said, "if Adams had patented his method."

The general raged at him. "And had it published, all neat and orderly, in the patent office records so that anyone who wanted it could look it up and have it?"

"We can be most sincerely thankful," said the chairman, "that he did not patent it."

VI

The helicopter would never fly again, but the time unit was intact.

Which didn't mean that it would work.

They held a powwow at their camp site. It had been, they decided, simpler to move the camp than to remove the body of Old Buster. So they had shifted at dawn, leaving the old mastodon still sprawled across the helicopter.

In a day or two, they knew, the great bones would be cleanly picked by the carrion birds, the lesser cats, the wolves and foxes and the little skulkers.

Getting the time unit out of the helicopter had been quite a chore, but they finally had managed and now Adams sat with it cradled in his lap.

"The worst of it," he told them, "is that I can't test it. There's no way to. You turn it on and it works or it doesn't work. You can't know till you try."

"That's something we can't help," Cooper replied. "The problem, seems to me, is how we're going to use it without the whirlybird."

"We have to figure out some way to get up in the air," said Adams. "We don't want to take the chance of going up into the twentieth century and arriving there about six feet underground."

"Common sense says that we should be higher here than up ahead," Hudson pointed out. "These hills have stood here since Jurassic times. They probably were a good deal higher then and have weathered down. That weathering still should be going on. So we should be higher here than in the twentieth century—not much, perhaps, but higher."

"Did anyone ever notice what the altimeter read?" asked Cooper.

"I don't believe I did," Adams admitted.

"It wouldn't tell you, anyhow," Hudson declared. "It would just give our height then and now—and we were moving, remember—and what about air pockets and relative atmosphere density and all the rest?"

Cooper looked as discouraged as Hudson felt.

"How does this sound?" asked Adams. "We'll build a platform twelve feet high. That certainly should be enough to clear us and yet small enough to stay within the range of the unit's force-field."

"And what if we're two feet higher here?" Hudson pointed out.

"A fall of fourteen feet wouldn't kill a man unless he's plain unlucky."

"It might break some bones."

"So it might break some bones. You want to stay here or take a chance on a broken leg?"

"All right, if you put it that way. A platform, you say. A platform out of what?"

"Timber. There's lot of it. We just go out and cut some logs."

"A twelve-foot log is heavy. And how are we going to get that big a log uphill?"

"We drag it."

"We try to, you mean."

"Maybe we could fix up a cart," said Adams, after thinking a moment.

"Out of what?" Cooper asked.

"Rollers, maybe. We could cut some and roll the logs up here."

"That would work on level ground," Hudson said. "It wouldn't work to roll a log uphill. It would get away from us. Someone might get killed."

"The logs would have to be longer than twelve feet, anyhow," Cooper put in. "You'd have to set them in a hole and that takes away some footage."

"Why not the tripod principle?" Hudson offered. "Fasten three logs at the top and raise them."

"That's a gin-pole, a primitive derrick. It'd still have to be longer than twelve feet. Fifteen, sixteen, maybe. And how are we going to hoist three sixteen-foot logs? We'd need a block and tackle."

"There's another thing," said Cooper. "Part of those logs might just be beyond the effective range of the force-field. Part of them would have to—*have to*, mind you—move in time and part couldn't. That would set up a stress. . . ."

"Another thing about it," added Hudson, "is that we'd travel with the logs. I don't want to come out in another time with a bunch of logs flying all around me."

"Cheer up," Adams told them. "Maybe the unit won't work, anyhow."

VII

The general sat alone in his office and held his head between his hands. The fools, he thought, the goddam knuckle-headed fools! Why couldn't they see it as clearly as he did?

For fifteen years now, as head of Project Mastodon, he had lived with it night and day and he could see all the possibilities as clearly as if they had been actual fact. Not military possibilities alone, although as a military man, he naturally would think of those first.

The hidden bases, for example, located within the very strong-holds of potential enemies—within, yet centuries removed in time. Many centuries removed and only seconds distant.

He could see it all: The materialization of the fleets; the swift, devastating blow, then the instantaneous retreat into the fastnesses of the past. Terrific destruction, but not a ship lost nor a man.

Except that if you had the bases, you need never strike the blow. If you had the bases and let the enemy know you had them, there would never be the provocation.

And on the home front, you'd have air-raid shelters that would be effective. You'd evacuate your population not in space, but time. You'd have the sure and absolute defense against any kind of bombing—fission, fusion, bacteriological or whatever else the labs had in stock.

And if the worst should come—which it never would with a setup like that—you'd have a place to which the entire nation could retreat, leaving to the enemy the empty, blasted cities and the lethally dusted countryside.

Sanctuary—that had been what Hudson had offered the then-secretary of state fifteen years ago—and the idiot had frozen up with the insult of it and had Hudson thrown out.

And if war did not come, think of the living space and the vast new opportunities—not the least of which would be the opportunity to achieve peaceful living in a virgin world, where the old hatreds would slough off and new concepts have a chance to grow.

He wondered where they were, those three who had gone back into time. Dead, perhaps. Run down by a mastodon. Or stalked by tigers. Or maybe done in by warlike tribesmen. No, he kept forgetting there weren't any in that era. Or trapped in time, unable to get back, condemned to exile in an alien time. Or maybe, he thought, just plain disgusted. And he couldn't blame them if they were.

Or maybe—let's be fantastic about this—sneaking in colonists from some place other than the watched Wisconsin farm, building up in actuality the nation they had claimed to be.

They had to get back to the present soon or Project Mastodon would be killed entirely. Already the research program had been halted and if something didn't happen quickly, the watch that was kept on the Wisconsin farm would be called off.

"And if they do that," said the general, "I know just what I'll do."

He got up and strode around the room.

"By God," he said, "I'll show 'em!"

VIII

It had taken ten full days of back-breaking work to build the pyramid. They'd hauled the rocks from the creek bed half a mile away and had piled them, stone by rolling stone, to the height of a full twelve feet. It took a lot of rocks and a lot of patience, for as the pyramid went up, the base naturally kept broadening out.

But now all was finally ready.

Hudson sat before the burned-out campfire and held his blistered hands before him.

It should work, he thought, better than the logs—and less dangerous.

Grab a handful of sand. Some trickled back between your fingers, but most stayed in your grasp. That was the principle of the pyramid of stones. When—and if—the time machine should work, most of the rocks would go along.

Those that didn't go would simply trickle out and do no harm. There'd be no stress or strain to upset the working of the force-field.

And if the time unit didn't work?

Or if it did?

This was the end of the dream, thought Hudson, no matter how you looked at it.

For even if they did get back to the twentieth century, there would be no money and with the film lost and no other taken to replace it, they'd have no proof they had traveled back beyond the dawn of history—back almost to the dawn of Man.

Although how far you traveled would have no significance. An hour or a million years would be all the same; if you could span the hour, you could span the million years. And if you could go back the million years, it was within your power to go back to the first tick of eternity, the first stir of time across the face of emptiness and nothingness—back to that initial instant when nothing as yet had happened or been planned or thought, when all the vastness of the Universe was a new slate waiting the first chalk stroke of destiny.

Another helicopter would cost thirty thousand dollars—and they didn't even have the money to buy the tractor that they needed to build the stockade.

There was no way to borrow. You couldn't walk into a bank and say you wanted thirty thousand to take a trip back to the Old Stone Age.

You still could go to some industry or some university or the government and if you could persuade them you had something on the ball—why, then, they might put up the cash after cutting themselves in on just about all of the profits. And, naturally, they'd run the show because it was their money and all you had done was the sweating and the bleeding.

"There's one thing that still bothers me," said Cooper, breaking the silence. "We spent a lot of time picking our spot so we'd miss the barn and house and all the other buildings. . . ."

"Don't tell me the windmill!" Hudson cried.

"No. I'm pretty sure we're clear of that. But the way I figure, we're right astraddle that barbed-wire fence at the south end of the orchard."

"If you want, we could move the pyramid over twenty feet or so."

Cooper groaned. "I'll take my chances with the fence." Adams got to his feet, the time unit tucked underneath his arm. "Come on, you guys. It's time to go."

They climbed the pyramid gingerly and stood unsteadily at its top.

Adams shifted the unit around, clasped it to his chest.

"Stand around close," he said, "and bend your knees a little. It may be quite a drop."

"Go ahead," said Cooper. "Press the button."

Adams pressed the button.

Nothing happened.

The unit didn't work.

IX

The chief of Central Intelligence was white-lipped when he finished talking.

"You're sure of your information?" asked the President.

"Mr. President," said the CIA chief, "I've never been more sure of anything in my entire life."

The President looked at the other two who were in the room, a question in his eyes.

The JCS chairman said, "It checks, sir, with everything we know."

"But it's incredible!" the President said.

"They're afraid," said the CIA chief. "They lie awake nights. They've become convinced that we're on the verge of traveling in time. They've tried and failed, but they think we're near success. To their way of thinking, they've got to hit us now or never, because once we actually get time travel, they know their number's up."

"But we dropped Project Mastodon entirely almost three years ago. It's been all of ten years since we stopped the research. It was twenty-five years ago that Hudson—"

"That makes no difference, sir. They're convinced we dropped the project publicly, but went underground with it. That would be the kind of strategy they could understand."

The President picked up a pencil and doodled on a pad.

"Who was that old general," he asked, "the one who raised so much fuss when we dropped the project? I remember I was in the Senate then. He came around to see me."

"Bowers, sir," said the JCS chairman.

"That's right. What became of him?"

"Retired."

"Well, I guess it doesn't make any difference now." He doodled some more and finally said, "Gentlemen, it looks like this is it. How much time did you say we had?"

"Not more than ninety days, sir. Maybe as little as thirty."

The President looked up at the JCS chairman.

"We're as ready," said the chairman, "as we will ever be. We can handle them—I think. There will, of course, be some—"

"I know," said the President.

"Could we bluff?" asked the secretary of state, speaking quietly. "I know it wouldn't stick, but at least we might buy some time."

"You mean hint that we have time travel?"

The secretary nodded.

"It wouldn't work," said the CIA chief tiredly. "If we really had it, there'd be no question then. They'd become exceedingly well-mannered, even neighborly, if they were sure we had it."

"But we haven't got it," said the President gloomily.

X

The two hunters trudged homeward late in the afternoon, with a deer slung from a pole they carried on their shoulders. Their breath hung visibly in the air as they walked along, for the frost had come and any day now, they knew, there would be snow.

"I'm worried about Wes," said Cooper, breathing heavily. "He's taking this too hard. We got to keep an eye on him."

"Let's take a rest," panted Hudson.

They halted and lowered the deer to the ground.

"He blames himself too much," said Cooper. He wiped his sweaty forehead. "There isn't any need to. All of us walked into this with our eyes wide open."

"He's kidding himself and he knows it, but it gives him something to go on. As long as he can keep busy with all his puttering around, he'll be all right."

"He isn't going to repair the time unit, Chuck."

"I know he isn't. And he knows it, too. He hasn't got the tools or the materials. Back in the workshop, he might have a chance, but here he hasn't."

"It's rough on him."

"It's rough on all of us."

"Yes, but we didn't get a brainstorm that marooned two old friends in this tail end of nowhere. And we can't make him swallow it when we say that it's okay, we don't mind at all."

"That's a lot to swallow, Johnny."

"What's going to happen to us, Chuck?"

"We've got ourselves a place to live and there's lots to eat. Save our ammo for the big game—a lot of eating for each bullet—and trap the smaller animals."

"I'm wondering what will happen when the flour and all the other stuff is gone. We don't have too much of it because we always figured we could bring in more."

"We'll live on meat," said Hudson. "We got bison by the million. The plains Indians lived on them alone. And in the spring, we'll find roots and in the summer berries. And in the fall, we'll harvest a half-dozen kinds of nuts."

"Some day our ammo will be gone, no matter how careful we are with it."

"Bows and arrows. Slingshots. Spears."

"There's a lot of beasts here I wouldn't want to stand up to with nothing but a spear."

"We won't stand up to them. We'll duck when we can and run when we can't duck. Without our guns, we're no lords of creation—not in this place. If we're going to live, we'll have to recognize that fact."

"And if one of us gets sick or breaks a leg or—"

"We'll do the best we can. Nobody lives forever."

But they were talking around the thing that really bothered them, Hudson told himself—each of them afraid to speak the thought aloud.

They'd live, all right, so far as food, shelter and clothing were concerned. And they'd live most of the time in plenty, for this was a fat and open-handed land and a man could make an easy living.

But the big problem—the one they were afraid to talk about— was their emptiness of purpose. To live, they had to find some meaning in a world without society.

A man cast away on a desert isle could always live for hope, but here there was no hope. A Robinson Crusoe was separated from his fellow-humans by, at the most, a few thousand miles. Here they were separated by a hundred and fifty thousand years.

Wes Adams was the lucky one so far. Even playing his thousand-to-one shot, he still held tightly to a purpose, feeble as it might be—the hope that he could repair the time machine.

We don't need to watch him now, thought Hudson. The time we'll have to watch is when he is forced to admit he can't fix the machine.

And both Hudson and Cooper had been kept sane enough, for there had been the cabin to be built and the winter's supply of wood to cut and the hunting to be done.

But then there would come a time when all the chores were finished and there was nothing left to do.

"You ready to go?" asked Cooper.

"Sure. All rested now," said Hudson.

They hoisted the pole to their shoulders and started off again.

Hudson had lain awake nights thinking of it and all the thoughts had been dead ends.

One could write a natural history of the Pleistocene, complete with photographs and sketches, and it would be a pointless thing to do, because no future scientist would ever have a chance to read it.

Or they might labor to build a memorial, a vast pyramid, perhaps, which would carry a message forward across fifteen hundred centuries, snatching with bare hands at a semblance of immortality. But if they did, they would be working against the sure and certain knowledge that it all would come to naught, for they knew in advance that no such pyramid existed in historic time.

Or they might set out to seek contemporary Man, hiking across four thousand miles of wilderness to Bering Strait and over into Asia. And having found contemporary Man cowering in his caves, they might be able to help him immeasurably along the road to his great inheritance. Except that they'd never make it and even if they did, contemporary Man undoubtedly would find some way to do them in and might eat them in the bargain.

They came out of the woods and there was the cabin, just a hundred yards away. It crouched against the hillside above the spring, with the sweep of grassland billowing beyond it to the slate-gray skyline. A trickle of smoke came up from the chimney and they saw the door was open.

"Wes oughtn't to leave it open that way," said Cooper. "No telling when a bear might decide to come visiting."

"Hey, Wes!" yelled Hudson.

But there was no sign of him.

Inside the cabin, a white sheet of paper lay on the table top. Hudson snatched it up and read it, with Cooper at his shoulder.

Dear guys—I don't want to get your hopes up again and have you disappointed. But I think I may have found the trouble. I'm going to try it out. If it doesn't work, I'll come back and burn this note and never say a word. But if you find the note, you'll know it worked and I'll be back to get you. Wes.

Hudson crumpled the note in his hand. "The crazy fool!"

"He's gone off his rocker," Cooper said. "He just thought. . . ."

The same thought struck them both and they bolted for the door. At the corner of the cabin, they skidded to a halt and stood there, staring at the ridge above them.

The pyramid of rocks they'd built two months ago was gone!

XI

The crash brought Gen. Leslie Bowers (ret.) up out of bed— about two feet out of bed—old muscles tense, white mustache bristling.

Even at his age, the general was a man of action. He flipped the covers back, swung his feet out to the floor and grabbed the shotgun leaning against the wall.

Muttering, he blundered out of the bedroom, marched across the dining room and charged into the kitchen. There, beside the door, he snapped on the switch that turned on the floodlights. He practically took the door off its hinges getting to the stoop and he stood there, bare feet gripping the planks, nightshirt billowing in the wind, the shotgun poised and ready.

"What's going on out there?" he bellowed.

There was a tremendous pile of rocks resting where he'd parked his car. One crumpled fender and a drunken headlight peeped out of the rubble.

A man was clambering carefully down the jumbled stones, making a detour to dodge the battered fender.

The general pulled back the hammer of the gun and fought to control himself.

The man reached the bottom of the pile and turned around to face him. The general saw that he was hugging something tightly to his chest.

"Mister," the general told him, "your explanation better be a good one. That was a brand-new car. And this was the first time I was set for a night of sleep since my tooth quit aching."

The man just stood and looked at him.

"Who in thunder are you?" roared the general.

The man walked slowly forward. He stopped at the bottom of the stoop.

"My name is Wesley Adams," he said. "I'm—"

"Wesley Adams!" howled the general. "My God, man, where have you been all these years?"

"Well, I don't imagine you'll believe me, but the fact is. . . ."

"We've been waiting for you. For twenty-five long years! Or, rather, *I've* been waiting for you. Those other idiots gave up. I've waited right here for you, Adams, for the last three years, ever since they called off the guard."

Adams gulped. "I'm sorry about the car. You see, it was this way. . . ."

The general, he saw, was beaming at him fondly.

"I had faith in you," the general said.

He waved the shotgun by way of invitation. "Come on in. I have a call to make."

Adams stumbled up the stairs.

"Move!" the general ordered, shivering. "On the double! You want me to catch my death of cold out here?"

Inside, he fumbled for the lights and turned them on. He laid the shotgun across the kitchen table and picked up the telephone.

"Give me the White House at Washington," he said. "Yes, I said the White House. . . . The President? Naturally he's the one I want to talk to. . . . Yes, it's all right. He won't mind my calling him."

"Sir," said Adams tentatively.

The general looked up. "What is it, Adams? Go ahead and say it."

"Did you say *twenty-five* years?"

"That's what I said. What were you doing all that time?"

Adams grasped the table and hung on. "But it wasn't. . . ."

"Yes," said the general to the operator. "Yes, I'll wait."

He held his hand over the receiver and looked inquiringly at Adams. "I imagine you'll want the same terms as before."

"Terms?"

"Sure. Recognition. Point Four Aid. Defense pact."

"I suppose so," Adams said.

"You got these saps across the barrel," the general told him happily. "You can get anything you want. You rate it, too, after what you've done and the bonehead treatment you got—but especially for not selling out."

XII

The night editor read the bulletin just off the teletype.

"Well, what do you know!" he said. "We just recognized Mastodonia."

He looked at the copy chief.

"Where the hell is Mastodonia?" he asked.

The copy chief shrugged. "Don't ask me. You're the brains in this joint."

"Well, let's get a map for the next edition," said the night editor.

XIII

Tabby, the saber-tooth, dabbed playfully at Cooper with his mighty paw.

Cooper kicked him in the ribs—an equally playful gesture.

Tabby snarled at him.

"Show your teeth at me, will you!" said Cooper. "Raised you from a kitten and that's the gratitude you show. Do it just once more and I'll belt you in the chops."

Tabby lay down blissfully and began to wash his face.

"Some day," warned Hudson, "that cat will miss a meal and that's the day you're it."

"Gentle as a dove," Cooper assured him. "Wouldn't hurt a fly."

"Well, one thing about it, nothing dares to bother us with that monstrosity around."

"Best watchdog there ever was. Got to have something to guard all this stuff we've got. When Wes gets back, we'll be millionaires. All those furs and ginseng and the ivory."

"*If* he gets back."

"He'll be back. Quit your worrying."

"But it's been five years," Hudson protested.

"He'll be back. Something happened, that's all. He's probably working on it right now. Could be that he messed up the time setting when he repaired the unit or it might have been knocked out of kilter when Buster hit the helicopter. That would take a while to fix. I don't worry that he won't come back. What I can't figure out is why did he go and leave us?"

"I've told you," Hudson said. "He was afraid it wouldn't work."

"There wasn't any need to be scared of that. We never would have laughed at him."

"No. Of course we wouldn't."

"Then what *was* he scared of?" Cooper asked.

"If the unit failed and we knew it failed, Wes was afraid we'd try to make him see how hopeless and insane it was. And he knew we'd probably convince him and then all his hope would be gone. And he wanted to hang onto that, Johnny. He wanted to hang onto his hope even when there wasn't any left."

"That doesn't matter now," said Cooper. "What counts is that he'll come back. I can feel it in my bones."

And here's another case, thought Hudson, of hope begging to be allowed to go on living.

God, he thought, I wish I could be that blind!

"Wes is working on it right now," said Cooper confidently.

XIV

He was. Not he alone, but a thousand others, working desperately, knowing that the time was short, working not alone for two men trapped in time, but for the peace they all had dreamed about—

that the whole world had yearned for through the ages.

For to be of any use, it was imperative that they could zero in the time machines they meant to build as an artilleryman would zero in a battery of guns, that each time machine would take its occupants to the same instant of the past, that their operation would extend over the same period of time, to the exact second.

It was a problem of control and calibration—starting with a prototype that was calibrated, as its finest adjustment, for jumps of 50,000 years.

Project Mastodon was finally under way.

ABOUT THE AUTHOR

Clifford D. Simak was born in Millville, Wisconsin in 1904. He attended the University of Wisconsin—Madison and later worked at various newspapers in the Midwest. He began a lifelong association with the *Minneapolis Star and Tribune* (Minneapolis, Minnesota) in 1939, which continued until his retirement in 1976. He became *Minneapolis Star*'s news editor in 1949 and coordinator of Minneapolis Tribune's Science Reading Series in 1961.

In a blurb in *Time and Again* he wrote: "I have been happily married to the same woman for thirty-three years and have two children. My favorite recreation is fishing (the lazy way, lying in a boat and letting them come to me). Hobbies: Chess, stamp collecting, growing roses." He dedicated the book to his wife Kay, "without whom I'd never have written a line". He was well liked by many of his science fiction cohorts, especially Isaac Asimov.

He was honored by fans with three Hugo awards and by colleagues with one Nebula award. He was also named the third Grand Master by the Science Fiction and Fantasy Writers of America in 1977. Among his best-known works are *Way Station*, *The Fellowship of the Talisman*, and *Project Pope*.

He died in Minneapolis in 1988.